"So w
office in
thought

Alex cocked his head to one side, his expression almost puzzled. "I didn't summon you in any *tone*. I asked if I could see you in my office. I even said please."

Casey softened. Poor Alex. Was it possible she was oversensitive, reverting to her old habit of looking for trouble as soon as someone got too close? "Well, maybe you just sounded . . . harried," she conceded.

"Or maybe it was something else entirely," Alex suggested with a disarming little grin.

"Such as?" she murmured, a telltale catch in her voice.

Alex curved his hands around her shoulders and drew her toward him. "Try . . . impatient."

"And—impulsive?" Casey ventured.

He reached up to cradle her face between his hands. "And impetuous."

Desire clouded Casey's eyes and a smile curved her lips.

"I have to leave for the airport in just a few minutes, and I need something from you before I go. Something important," Alex added.

"What . . . would that be?" Casey asked, though she had a fairly good idea.

"This, of course," Alex murmured as he dipped his head and covered her lips with his. Casey was intoxicated instantly, her senses reeling from the taste of Alex's mouth, her imagination fired by the brush of his tongue, her body aching for his. . . .

WHAT ARE *LOVESWEPT* ROMANCES?

They are stories of true romance and touching emotion. We believe those two very important ingredients are constants in our highly sensual and very believable stories in the *LOVESWEPT* line. Our goal is to give you, the reader, stories of consistently high quality that may sometimes make you laugh, sometimes make you cry, but are always fresh and creative and contain many delightful surprises within their pages.

Most romance fans read an enormous number of books. Those they truly love, they keep. Others may be traded with friends and soon forgotten. We hope that each *LOVESWEPT* romance will be a treasure—a "keeper." We will always try to publish

LOVE STORIES YOU'LL NEVER FORGET
BY AUTHORS YOU'LL ALWAYS REMEMBER

The Editors

Loveswept ® 511

Gail Douglas
After Hours

BANTAM BOOKS
NEW YORK · TORONTO · LONDON · SYDNEY · AUCKLAND

AFTER HOURS

A Bantam Book / December 1991

*If you would be interested in receiving protective vinyl
covers for your Loveswept books, please write to this address
for information:*

*Loveswept
Bantam Books
P.O. Box 985
Hicksville, NY 11802*

ISBN 0-553-44154-X

Published simultaneously in the United States and Canada

*Bantam Books are published by Bantam Books, a division of
Bantam Doubleday Dell Publishing Group, Inc. Its trademark,
consisting of the words "Bantam Books" and the portrayal of a
rooster, is Registered in U.S. Patent and Trademark Office and
in other countries. Marca Registrada. Bantam Books, 666
Fifth Avenue, New York, New York 10103.*

PRINTED IN THE UNITED STATES OF AMERICA

OPM   0 9 8 7 6 5 4 3 2 1

To Jane, who was the first to know.

One

Casey McIntyre stood deadly still behind the closed door of *The Vancouver Weekender*'s deserted composing room, holding a thick dictionary over her head.

Casey thought she was alone in the rambling old mansion that housed the small newspaper's offices, but someone had just joined her—someone, she was certain, who had no business being there at eleven o'clock at night. A *Webster's Unabridged* didn't seem like much of a weapon for warding off a burglar, but she was ready to slam it down on the intruder's head with all her might the instant he opened the door and stepped into the room.

Casey wished she hadn't started thinking about *The Shining*. About Jack Nicholson's diabolical grin. About how easy it was to shatter a door with an ax. She wished she hadn't found it necessary to work late in a Bates Motel of a building that stimulated her too-fertile imagination even in broad daylight. She wished . . . dammit, she wished the break-in artist would hurry up and make his move! Nothing could be worse than this suspense!

Come and get it, she said silently, whipping up her courage as she watched the doorknob slowly turning. *Come on, you. . .*

The door opened, and Casey realized too late that she'd made a serious tactical error. She was tall—taller than most men—an advantage she'd been counting on, along with the element of surprise. But the intruder had at least four inches on her and obviously had been ready for her sneak attack. He'd manacled her wrists with his strong fingers and pinned her to the wall with the weight of his body before she could even come close to conking him on the head.

"Who the hell are you, and what are you doing here?" he questioned in a menacing voice as Casey stared up at him in stunned dismay. "What are you up to?"

"What am *I* doing here?" she said on a sharp intake of breath, more taken aback then frightened. "What am *I* up to?"

"I also asked who you are, lady, so start talking."

Casey's jaw dropped. The utter gall of the man! She tried a knee-to-the-groin maneuver to give him a hint of how outraged she was, but it didn't work. She couldn't move her leg—or much of anything else. She was trapped, utterly immobile, and acutely aware of how vulnerable she was as she felt the powerful male chest and thighs pressed into her.

She closed her mouth and studied her attacker, hoping to spot some weakness she could take advantage of. But as she took in his dark wavy hair, blazing blue eyes, chiseled features, and sleek gray suit, she not only didn't find a weakness, she forgot to search for one. Good lord, he was gorgeous! What kind of burglar was he, anyway? How dare a man who looked like a television idol be a petty hoodlum?

"Well?" he asked.

"I'm Casey McIntyre, the assistant editor of this newspaper, and I'm here because I'm working overtime," she snapped out. Something was all wrong, she realized. *He* was the intruder; why was *she* the one submitting to the third degree? She decided to try to gain the upper hand by changing tactics. Pasting on a phony smile, she said sweetly, "But enough about me. Let's talk about you. Who are you, what are you doing here, and what, exactly, is your game?"

"I'm Alex McLean," he said, his tone less angry but still dubious, a quizzical smile twitching at the corners of his mouth.

Casey's eyes widened. "Alex McLean?" she said with a gasp. "*Our* Alex McLean?"

He raised one dark brow. "I hadn't thought of myself as anybody's Alex McLean, but I do own this paper, if that's what you mean."

"You can't be," Casey said flatly, recovering her wits. "You're out of town. I mean . . . *he* is."

"Are you sure?" Alex said, the reluctant smile finally taking hold. "Obviously you don't know the man at all. Odd, an assistant editor not knowing her publisher."

Casey tilted her head to one side and studied him again, this time determined to keep her wayward thoughts on the facts at hand. "Okay, I've never met Mr. McLean, but that's because I started here just after he left on a business trip a couple of weeks ago," she conceded aloud. Then she remembered a crucial set of details. "But he sent a fax from Calgary late this afternoon, and it so happens there's a wildcat strike at the airport there, which means he couldn't possibly be back in Vancouver."

"Haven't you heard of private planes and noncommercial landing strips?" he asked, his smile broadening. "Of friends, pardon my pun, in high places? A buddy with a Cessna was heading this way, so I hitched a ride."

Casey felt the blood drain from her face. "Oh-oh," she murmured.

To his amazement Alex found he had to suppress a chuckle as he watched the truth sink in. "You seem more worried now than when you thought I was a burglar."

"Yes, well . . ." Casey rolled her eyes toward the dictionary she still held and shook her head in defeat. "I've been known to have run-ins with publishers, but this has to be some kind of record." She smiled tentatively and wondered what was going to happen now.

All at once Alex was conscious of the full breasts, trim hips, and long, slender thighs crushed against his body with a fit as perfect as interlocking jigsaw-puzzle pieces. Heat started curling through him like smoke from the embers of a fire that was stirring to life again.

He tried to ignore the tiny flares of desire shooting to every recess and extremity of his being. His reaction was natural, he told himself. After all, he was a healthy male pressed full-length against a tall, green-eyed, luscious strawberry blond. But the fire would die out if he smothered it instead of fanning the flames. And he would definitely smother it. He'd had enough of that brand of trouble. He didn't need any more, at least right now. He had other things on his mind.

"Perhaps . . ." Casey managed a stiff smile. "Perhaps you'd consider . . . um . . ." She peered upward. "My wrists . . . ?"

Good idea, Alex thought, becoming aware only at

that moment that he still held Casey captive. He knew he should let her go. It would help him cool down a little. But he hesitated. "Will you promise not to throw the book at me?" he asked, realizing that he was making a dumb joke for the express purpose of stalling. So much for iron discipline.

Casey laughed softly. "I promise."

Alex hesitated again, his gaze drawn to her sweetly curved lips. He didn't think he'd ever seen such a delectable mouth. Full and soft and pink, it was made to be tasted and explored at a man's leisure. What if he indulged in just a . . . ?

Let her go! he commanded himself. There was no excuse for holding her so that the warmth of her breath on his skin, her musky feminine fragrance, could tease his senses.

But he didn't let her go. He didn't want to. Not when his lips were almost touching hers and he could feel the quick rise and fall of her breasts against his chest. Oh, he was willing to set her wrists free, but only so he could let his hands glide slowly down the tender underside of her arms, then . . .

Cool it, McLean, he thought desperately. He had to do something. His libido's thermostat was surging toward the danger zone. *Just cool it. Now.*

"Mr. McLean?" Casey said in a small voice, suspecting she was on the verge of being kissed and wanting it to happen—with a perfect stranger. Her publisher, no less! They hadn't taught her how to handle this situation back in Journalism 101. "I won't bounce my dictionary off your head," she assured him breathlessly. "You can trust me."

Alex blinked, uncurled his fingers, and very reluctantly stepped back, his glance making a quick perusal of the lithe, lush figure under Casey McIntyre's short-sleeve pink T-shirt and faded denims. He wanted her. He'd never felt such instant, powerful desire. Worse, he liked her. He didn't know Casey at all, yet his every instinct was drawn to her, if only because her feistiness appealed to him. But trust? That was another matter. "Suppose you tell me why you're here alone at this hour?" he said tersely, taking the dictionary from her and placing it on a nearby shelf.

Casey rubbed her wrists and returned to stand behind her worktable, using it as a barricade. She wished she hadn't gone home at six to change to her most comfortable clothes for working alone. If she'd worn a bra, she might feel a bit less vulnerable. Not that she had any reason to worry, she thought perversely as Alex McLean stood glowering at her. At the moment he didn't appear the least bit interested in what she was or wasn't wearing. A heartbeat earlier he'd seemed ready to devour her, but now he looked as if she ranked somewhere below fried porridge on his list of preferences. "I'm doing the paste-up for this Saturday's paper," she answered when she could make her tone as matter-of-fact as his.

"This is Thursday night. Ron Coulter does pasteup on Friday mornings."

"Not this week, Mr. McLean. Ron turned green early this afternoon and went home to his sickbed— or to the hospital, if he took my advice. I told him I could handle things here."

"And can you?" Alex asked quietly.

"I wouldn't have said so if I couldn't," Casey answered with more bravado than conviction.

Alex watched as she picked up her X-Acto knife and deftly sliced away the excess paper around a column of type. It was tempting to take the girl at face value—especially when she had such a lovely face— but he'd been burned too often lately, on too many fronts. He didn't take anything at face value. "I still don't know why you're here this late," he said, deciding to have a look at what she'd done so far. He hoped he wouldn't find what he'd discovered the last time he'd checked up on an assistant editor in the composing room after hours. Would he see that Casey, like her predecessor, was working against him rather than for him? It seemed hard to believe that his enemy—or enemies —would attempt the same cheap stunt twice, but they might be clumsy enough to take another stab at it.

Casey refused to look at her boss as he approached her work area. His invasion of her space was unnerving, but there wasn't much she could say. It was actually his space.

"You're a little slow with your answers," Alex said as he hooked his toe around the leg of a stool and dragged it over so he could sit down and go through the pages she'd completed.

Still standing as she bent over her work, Casey frowned in puzzlement. She was so distracted by Alex McLean's impact on her, she had no idea what answer he was waiting for. After searching her mind in vain, she admitted, "I don't remember what you asked me."

"Why you're here at this hour," Alex said absently, spot-checking ads for anything that looked suspicious.

"Oh, right." Casey heaved a deep sigh and realized she had to tell him the truth. It was too bad the top brass had caught her red-handed, but those things happened. She might as well make a clean breast of it. "Okay, I confess."

Alex's head snapped up. *I confess.* Why did those two words from this particular woman make his stomach twist into a knot? "I'm listening," he said after a pause of a few beats.

Casey sighed again, feeling foolish about being caught in a bluff. "I didn't have any choice," she said defensively. "Ron was really sick, and since one of the three production people happens to be off for the summer, and the other two are swamped, I said I could take care of the editorial pages that Ron usually does. I meant it too. I just didn't say . . . how long it might take me." She hesitated, then added, "I do know what I'm doing, but I'm a little rusty, so I wanted to get a head start."

Alex felt his insides unclenching. "That's your confession?" he asked softly. "That's it?"

Turning her head to face him at last, Casey watched his tense features relax, and she wondered what he'd been braced for. "Isn't it bad enough that I told your managing editor I was competent to go solo when most of the pasteup hours I've logged in the past were for an underground tabloid in college, a full nine years ago?"

Alex gazed into her green eyes and believed her. Just like that, he believed her. Maybe there was something in the air, he mused. Perhaps Casey's delicious fragrance had some component that numbed the suspicious area of his brain.

Forcing himself to continue studying the completed pages, he found nothing wrong. "Judging by what you've done so far, Casey, you seem competent enough to me."

"You really think so, Mr. McLean?" she asked, pleasantly surprised by his verdict.

He looked up and saw the corners of Casey's mouth tilt upward, and a gentle warmth spread through him that was even more unnerving than the heat he'd experienced moments before. "The name's Alex, and yes, I do think so," he said, his voice gruff as he dragged his gaze away from her again. Trouble, he thought. The woman was short-circuiting his common sense. Perhaps it was the excitement over how they'd met, but he was feeling things he had no business feeling. He knew he had to get out of there—and fast. He couldn't be certain of his self-control. "There's no need for you to stay any later tonight," he said as he got to his feet.

Casey shook her head and smiled. "Oh, but there is. Unless I allow myself plenty of time, I can't count on having the flats ready for proofreading by noon tomorrow. But it's no problem for me to stay another hour or so. I'm a night owl."

"Forgive another bad pun, but I don't give a hoot what your nocturnal habits are," Alex said, striding toward the door. "You're going home now, and that's all there is to it. I'll give you a hand with the rest of the pages in the morning."

"But you're just . . ." Casey stopped short, horrified at what she'd almost said.

"Just a publisher?" Alex finished helpfully, resting his hand on the doorknob as he turned to grin at her.

A crimson warmth swept over Casey's cheeks. "I didn't say that."

"No, you caught yourself in the nick of time. But it's what you were thinking. You've pegged me as a businessman, not a newspaperman."

"That's not quite so," Casey protested. "It's obvious to anybody who reads the papers in your chain that you're interested in a lot more than the bottom line on a balance sheet. It's just that . . ."

"That you share the typical journalist's prejudice against publishers in general," Alex cut in pleasantly. "You figure we're accountants or ad salesmen, and the farther away we stay from the nitty-gritty of putting a paper to bed, the better. We just get in the way, right?"

Burning with embarrassment, Casey gave a strained little laugh. "Right," she admitted, wondering if she was writing her own pink slip.

Alex glanced at a brass coatrack by the door and saw a black leather jacket on one of the hooks. "Yours?" he asked.

"Yes, but . . ."

"Don't argue with me, Casey," he said, moving to get the jacket and hold it out for her. "The party's over for tonight. What's more, I don't want you working alone in here again."

She frowned, none too pleased by such orders. She'd moved all the way from Ottawa to Vancouver and had taken a temporary but giant career step backward for the sake of learning things she needed to know—things about the way she wanted to live, things to help her reach her long-term goals, things about the country she'd grown up in but had seen too little of. Not things like jumping to obey commands as if she were some scared army recruit. "You're a pretty bossy individual," she commented, putting her hands on her hips and not budging.

Alex's smile didn't waver. "It's my privilege. I'm the boss."

"Ron told me you didn't interfere in the day-to-day operations of your papers. He's the managing editor, and he trusted me to do the job. I think I should stay and do it."

Gripped by an insane urge to go back over to Casey and take her in his arms to show her just where her stubbornness was liable to lead, Alex checked the impulse. "It's true that I don't interfere with the day-to-day issues," he conceded, then added with a deliberate caress in his voice, "The ones at night, however, are another matter." Satisfied to see Casey's eyes darken and a flush creep over her skin, he switched to a more businesslike tone. "Besides, I try to stay out of a managing editor's way, but a brand-new, basically untried assistant editor is a whole other matter. Now let's get a move on. I'm running out of patience."

"Fine," Casey snapped, knowing she had no choice but to give in. Tidying up her work area with abrupt, angry movements, she realized she was deeply shaken by Alex McLean—the man as well as the publisher—and her susceptibility annoyed her almost as much as his overbearing manner did. "After all, you *are* the boss." She marched toward him, turned, and thrust her arms into her jacket sleeves.

Somehow Alex managed not to wrap his arms around her, haul her back against him, and bury his face in the perfumed cloud of her hair or nuzzle her ear the way he longed to. With enormous self-discipline he simply stood aside and let Casey precede him through the doorway, then followed her and quickly locked the door behind them.

He didn't blame Casey for her little fit of pique. He was being awfully autocratic. But his insistence on leaving was a matter of self-defense. The woman was irresistible and didn't seem to know it—which made her all the more appealing. Her leather jacket emphasized rather than undermined her femininity, and as he watched her walking ahead of him, he was amazed how alluring jeans could be even when they weren't skintight. He didn't dare spend another moment alone with her. There was no room on his crowded agenda for getting involved with any female, much less somebody on his staff.

They reached the building's main entrance and went out into the crisp night air. As Alex paused to lock the door, he asked, "Do you live nearby, Casey, or could you use a lift home? My car's out back."

"I can walk," she answered, her tone frosty. "My place is just a few blocks away, near Stanley Park. And I thought yours was right upstairs. Why are you locking yourself out?"

"Because I'm going to walk you home," he said pleasantly.

"My apartment's no more than five minutes from here," Casey insisted, heading down the steps and striding along the sidewalk. "There's no need for you to walk me home."

Alex kept pace with her. "Casey, I've already told you not to bother arguing with me. If I decide I'm going to walk you home, prepare to be escorted to your door." He lightened his tone as he added, "It's been said, with some justification, that I'm a little bullheaded." Also uncompromising, self-centered, and unrealistic, he added silently. He had the official documents that said so.

"You do have definite dictator tendencies," Casey muttered, trying her best to sound disgruntled as Alex took her hand and tucked it under his arm. She couldn't help being glad he was bullheaded in this instance—though she wasn't about to admit it. "But far be it from me to rebel," she added theatrically. "I know my place."

Alex merely laughed. "Now you're catching on. Maybe you and I will get along after all."

"I wouldn't bet on it, boss. I'd say my days at *The Weekender* are numbered, which is pretty disappointing, because I think it's a real privilege to work for one of the best weeklies I've ever run across, even if a few indignities like sneak attacks in the composing room and taking orders from a tyrant go with the territory."

Alex was warmed by her words. He was proud of his newspapers, especially *The Weekender*, his flagship operation. It pleased him inordinately that Casey thought he was doing a good job—though he had no idea if she was qualified to judge.

Suddenly Casey stopped dead. "Why *did* you attack me so fiercely?"

Drawing to a halt Alex turned to smile regretfully at her. He'd been hoping she wouldn't ask that question. Not yet, anyway. He couldn't think clearly with Casey around, and he wasn't sure at this point how much he wanted to tell her. "It's a long story," he said after a moment. "What it boils down to is that I caught our last assistant editor making changes to some pasted-up flats after hours one night, and I had to fire him. I thought maybe someone had found a way to continue his efforts while I was supposed to be out of town."

Casey scowled as she lapsed into deep thought, then brightened so suddenly, Alex could almost see the light bulb over her head. "That explains it!"

Alex raised his brows, wondering what she could have figured out so quickly. "Explains what?"

"The errors. The little inaccuracies that gradually turned into glaring mistakes. Good heavens, all this time I was thinking I'd gotten this job because of the last person's incompetence, and the truth was you were being sabotaged! But why, for heaven's sake? I mean, this is the neighborhood weekly market, not . . ." Casey frowned again. "Still, when a paper comes out swinging in its editorials, dives into controversial issues, and names names the way yours does, you're bound to make some nasty enemies. But really, sabotage? It's so melodramatic."

Mind-boggling, Alex thought. It was nothing short of mind-boggling the way this woman had figured everything out in a matter of seconds. Was she that brilliant—or did she know something?

His impulsive decision to trust Casey wavered. "How did you get the picture so fast?" he asked bluntly.

"I've done some homework," she answered, beginning to walk again. "I've read a pile of back issues of *The Weekender,* and I noticed the gradual problems that started just after you'd announced hiring an assistant editor and ended just before you advertised for a new one—namely me, as it turned out. As I said, I figured somebody else's incompetence was my opportunity. Not for a moment did I imagine anyone would play such dirty tricks. That stuff's for big business and politics, not little newspapers."

Alex laughed and shook his head, regretting that he'd doubted Casey even for a moment. Her explanation made perfect sense. In her place he'd have done the same kind of homework, noticed the same problems, and ultimately reached the same conclusions. "You sound more like a detective than a journalist," he said teasingly.

"The line between the two is pretty fuzzy sometimes," she commented. "To get back to this case, are you still having troubles?"

"I'm still having troubles, but I guess I didn't really think. I just reacted."

"What kind of troubles?"

Alex smiled, but shook his head. "Casey, it's nearly midnight. You're tired, I'm beat, and we have a paper to get out tomorrow. Maybe there'll be time for me to explain the gory details after we get the pasteup finished, but for now let's not talk shop, all right?"

Deciding he still didn't trust her, Casey shrugged and gave him a forced smile. "Like I said, Alex, you're the boss."

The remainder of the walk to Casey's apartment somehow managed to seem both endless and fleeting, and the stream of meaningless banter she and Alex indulged in struck her as having more to do with trying *not* to get to know each other than with becoming acquainted.

The only piece of basic information she gleaned about Alex was that he'd grown up in Vancouver—in the West End, in fact, a couple of blocks north of the beautiful curve of English Bay. And the most confidential tidbit she shared with him was that she'd arrived on the west coast just six weeks before. She told him May had been a perfect month for a cross-country drive. That was about as personal as it got between them.

The near kiss of less than an hour ago might never have happened.

Apparently, Casey mused, she'd met her match when it came to being wary. But that was fine with her. She had no interest in the complications that went with even the mildest male-female attraction. No interest whatsoever.

As they walked, Casey was surprised by the number of people who spoke to Alex, from owners of after-hours stores to cops on the beat, from boisterous teenagers on summer vacation to derelicts who greeted him by name before thrusting out their palms for the change he readily dropped into them. Guarded as Alex was with her, he seemed to be a regular Good Neighbor Sam with everyone else. It was as if the West End was a country village, and Alex was its long time mayor.

When they reached her apartment building and Alex insisted on seeing her right to her door, Casey took his earlier advice about not arguing. She wasn't used to such protectiveness; it wasn't the kind of thing she normally inspired in men. She was surprised to feel an odd little glow spread through her.

She found herself thinking again about kisses, wondering to her utter amazement whether Alex was going to kiss her—try to kiss her, she amended hastily. She, of course, wouldn't dream of letting it happen.

But Alex didn't try to kiss her.

Casey said a prim good night to him, and he responded with an offhand salute over his shoulder as he strolled down the hallway toward the elevator.

Well, Casey thought as she let herself into her furnished bachelor unit, she certainly was relieved he was such a perfect gentleman. Relieved beyond belief.

What she couldn't understand was why she'd allowed herself to dwell on something as unlikely, adolescent, and unacceptable as a good-night kiss from her publisher. It wasn't her style at all. And he hadn't exactly built her up to a state of anticipation during their walk.

The whole thing was crazy, not to mention totally out of character. She'd always been the buddy type, caught by surprise and usually disappointed when a man started turning mushy on her. She didn't go around thinking about kisses. Half expecting kisses. *Hoping* for them, dammit!

Closing the door and leaning back against it, Casey laughed at herself and touched her fingertips to her lips. They were tingling and felt slightly swollen as if . . .

Oh lord, she thought as her laughter faded, what kind of trouble had she gotten herself into when she'd accepted this job?

She could deal with interlopers who were determined to create problems for the paper. Sleazy operators were an unfortunate part of doing business these days.

What she wasn't sure she was ready for—what she'd never been trained to handle—was a saboteur of the heart.

Two

The pewter sky over English Bay was streaked with the pinks and lavenders of sunrise when Casey strode into The Starting Gate, an unpretentious diner run by an ex-jockey who opened every morning at six for the early-bird crowd—and the bleary-eyed, night-prowling denizens who were just about to call it a day.

An early-morning pit stop at The Starting Gate was one of the first routines Casey had established once she'd moved to the west coast. Her childhood friend Brittany Thomas had made the Ottawa-to-Vancouver plunge six months earlier, and her letters about life in Canada's Lotus Land had finally persuaded Casey to pull up stakes. Brittany had taken great pride in showing off the down-home hospitality of the little café the first time she and Casey had met there.

"'Morning, Smiley," Casey greeted the wiry, beak-nosed owner as she settled onto a stool at the long white counter.

"Hiya, Strawberry. You're the first customer of the day," he said with a tip of his jockey cap as he looked up from his racing form with the ear-to-ear grin that had earned him his nickname. Like a Damon Runyon character straight out of *Guys and Dolls*, Smiley instantly renamed almost everybody he encountered. "Cookie's not here yet," he added unnecessarily. Brittany had earned her moniker by having one oatmeal cookie and a glass of milk for breakfast every day.

Casey smiled as she scanned the chalkboard list of the morning's offerings. "Britt will be along any minute," she said absently. "I'm a bit early."

Smiley peered more closely at Casey as he set a mug of black coffee on the counter in front of her. "Didn't sleep well last night?"

Observant fellow, Casey thought, almost afraid Smiley was looking into her eyes and seeing the erotic images that had kept her awake most of the night. "What kind of muffin should I try?" she asked in an effort to distract him.

He gave her a knowing smile, clearly recognizing her ploy for what it was. "Well, the wife's pretty proud of the pumpkin ones. Says they're low fat, low cal . . . whatever all that mumbo jumbo is. You want to try one?"

"I'd love to," Casey answered eagerly. Hearing the diner's door open, she looked back over her shoulder and saw Brittany sailing in, dressed in a multicolored tracksuit much like Casey's, her chestnut hair pulled carelessly up into a topknot that bounced as she moved.

"Just how late did you work last night?" Brittany asked as she plunked herself down on the stool beside Casey. "I called you at eleven, and you still weren't home."

"Eleven? I'd just finished about that time," Casey answered with a grin. Brittany was such a little mother hen—all five feet three of her. "And what were you doing up at that hour? You're usually tucked in by ten—unless you've changed your habits since college."

"A Lion's Club function at the hotel ran late," Brittany explained with a shrug. "I felt I should stay till the bitter end."

Smiley delivered Casey's pumpkin muffin, then put a chilled glass of milk and a still-warm-from-the-oven oatmeal cookie in front of Brittany. "Both you girls work too hard," he scolded, completely unselfconscious about joining their conversation. He did it with everybody, as if he felt he had a perfect right to be part of any socializing that was going on in his place. No one ever objected—Smiley was Smiley. "What are you trying to do?" he went on. "Become millionaires before you're thirty?"

"It's too late," Brittany said. "We both hit the big three-oh this year, and I don't think either one of us is close to the first million."

"Not yet, anyway," Casey added optimistically. "But who are you to talk, Smiley? You and Ruby work longer hours than the two of us put together."

"That's different. We love it," he argued. "This diner's not just a living, it's our life."

"That's how I feel about my job at The Somerset," Brittany said.

"And I'm the same way about *The Weekender*," Casey claimed, though she was stretching things a bit. She definitely wasn't building a life at that newspaper, or even a career with Alex's company. She was serving an apprenticeship and would be moving on as soon as the time was right. But she did love the work.

Another pair of customers arrived, and when Smiley went to take care of them, Brittany turned to Casey. "How did the pasteup go?"

"So-so," Casey answered. She took a tentative bite of her muffin.

Brittany contentedly munched away on her cookie. "What do you mean, so-so? Did you run into problems?" she asked between bites.

"Well, I was moving along slowly, when Alex McLean got back early from his trip." Casey saw that Smiley was still busy at the other end of the counter, so she proceeded to regale Brittany with the details of the way she'd met her new publisher. She didn't, however, mention the powerful and conflicting feelings Alex had aroused in her. They were too disturbing to discuss, even with her closest friend. "So the upshot is," she said as she finished her tale, "Alex escorted me home whether I wanted to leave or not. He said he'd help me put the rest of the pages together."

"That's nice," Brittany said complacently. "It's not every publisher who'd pitch in that way."

"Nice? Hey, Britt, don't you realize I'm ticked off? The man treated me like a teenager caught breaking curfew. I just hope Alex will be more help than hindrance," Casey said. "I've been studying Ron Coulter's layout style. To have someone else involved will probably just confuse me."

"Oh, I'm sure Alex knows what he's doing," Brittany commented. "He doesn't strike me as the type who'd say he could handle something he couldn't."

Casey's eyes widened as the implication in Brittany's words hit home. "Good grief, does everybody know that man? Or is this neighborhood even more of a small town than I'd realized?"

"It's not so much the neighborhood as the work Alex and I do," Brittany said. "Hotel people and media types tend to run into one another at press conferences and so on. And I don't really know him all that well. It's more of a nodding acquaintance."

"Hey, is Scoop back from his trip?" Smiley put in, bringing over the coffeepot to give Casey a refill.

Casey laughed and rolled her eyes. Scoop, she assumed, was Alex. "You know him too?"

"Of course I do, Strawberry. I know everybody in this town—in this part of it, anyhow. So does Scoop. Besides, he eats here at least three times a week unless he's on the road keeping tabs on the rest of his papers, and my Ruby has known him since he was a kid. She's always lived in the West End. same as Scoop has. He's a good man. Hate to see him go under."

Casey almost choked on her muffin. "Go under?" she repeated when she'd pulled herself together. "What do you mean?"

"Well, it could be just talk, but a couple of junior accountants were in here a few days ago playing hooky on an hour-long coffee break and shooting their mouths off trying to impress each other. One of them claimed that *The Weekender* is going to fold before the year's out. I've been waiting for Scoop to come in so I could tell him what they said. I don't like squealing on my customers, but I figure these guys were yakking out of turn, so all bets are off." He shrugged. "Besides, they're not regulars."

Casey was too stunned to respond. She stared off into space, as startled by the sick feeling washing over her as by what Smiley had told her.

"I find it hard to believe Alex's company could be in trouble," Brittany said quietly. "*The Weekender* is enormously popular, and getting more so all the time. I'm sure your job is safe, Casey—"

"I'm not worried about my job," Casey said without a moment's hesitation. "I'm concerned about—" She stopped abruptly, realizing she'd almost blurted out that she was concerned about Alex. And she was. The man had bullied her, had made it perfectly clear he didn't trust her, and had ruined her night's sleep. And what was her response? Her very first response when her job was threatened? She cared what happened to *him*. She wanted to *protect* Alex McLean, for heaven's sake! Well, she might be idiotic enough to feel that way, but she didn't have to admit it. "I'm concerned about the paper," she said carefully. "It's performing a valuable service in this neighborhood, and it would be a shame to lose it."

"If it's any comfort," Smiley said, "I didn't get the impression these guys really had any inside info. They were passing on something they'd heard." He shook his head in disgust. "I don't know what's happened to ethics these days. I'm telling you, the whole world's getting to be as sleazy as the track at its worst."

Casey fell silent, mentally reviewing the few disturbing facts she had at her fingertips: An editor had tried to mess up the paper; Alex had admitted there'd been other problems; financial types were spreading the word that he had money troubles, a sure-fire way to *give* him money troubles. Advertisers could be very skittish about newspapers that might not be around long.

But the story didn't make sense, Casey reasoned. *The Weekender* was pulling in plenty of ads, and surely the revenue from them would keep the company in good shape. Something wasn't ringing true, and she was going to find out what it was. "Smiley, is it okay with you if I pass on to Alex what you told me?" she asked with sudden urgency.

"Go right ahead. And if he wants to see me about it, I'll tell him exactly what was said. I'll try to find out who the young pups were too. They were crazy about Ruby's deep-dish apple pie, and I think they work around here somewhere. They'll probably be back soon."

"Thanks, Smiley," Casey said. As he moved to take care of a red-faced jogger who'd staggered into the diner, she turned to Brittany. "Do you mind if I skip our morning walk, Britt? I want to get a jump on the rest of the pasteup so I can take time to talk to Alex later this morning about all this."

"Go right ahead," Brittany said, obviously suppressing a mischievous smile. "But what's happening here? Is our own Brenda Starr sensing a story of some kind, or was there more to your first meeting with Alex than you mentioned? Now that I think about it, he *is* pretty dishy."

"Now that you think about it?" Casey repeated, astonished. "You have to think about it?"

Brittany's smile broke through. "To each her own, Case. Alex is too intense for my taste. From what I know of the man, he's charming, quick-witted, community minded, and nice to look at. But there's something about him that would make me hesitate to get too close. It's almost as if there's something seething under his pleasant veneer. I don't think I'd want to be around if all that pent-up energy ever exploded."

Casey laughed off Brittany's words and quickly finished her muffin and coffee, said her good-byes, and raced home to dress for the office.

She'd wear the black-and-white houndstooth linen jacket and black skirt, she decided as she glanced through her closet, with high heels and a bright blouse. After being caught the way she'd looked the night before, she wanted to show Alex that she was capable of looking stylishly professional, even for doing pasteup.

All the way to the newspaper she couldn't stop

thinking about the restless volcano churning so close to Alex's surface that even Brittany had noticed it.

Yet instead of wanting to keep a safe distance, Casey found herself shivering with anticipation at the thought of being nearby when the eruption occurred.

Good lord, she thought. She was in even bigger trouble than she'd realized.

Casey had hung up her jacket and was seated at the layout table in *The Weekender*'s composing room by seven o'clock, determined to finish the pasteup before Alex arrived at nine—partly to prove she could do the job on her own, but mostly to free them both for the heart-to-heart talk she was determined they were going to have.

Alex walked in at five after seven. "I had a feeling I'd better get down here early," he said, standing inside the open doorway with his feet astride, one hand resting loosely on his hips as he did his best to glare at Casey.

He chose not to tell her that he'd been up for two hours, waiting to hear the building's main door creaking open and shut, eager to see his new assistant editor and secretly hoping she would flout his orders of the night before. "I thought we agreed that you wouldn't work alone in here again, Casey," he said, satisfied that he sounded stern.

Casey glanced at Alex long enough to take in the way the rolled-up sleeves and open collar of his white shirt revealed a tantalizing glimpse of tanned skin and dark chest hair, emphasizing his masculinity in an extremely unsettling way.

Swallowing hard she hastily returned her attention to the page she was working on. "Good morning, boss," she said when she'd caught her breath, hoping she appeared cooler than she felt. "I haven't been alone."

"Oh? Who's been with you? One of the local squirrels?"

Casey looked up again, this time to flash him a quick impish grin. "No. One of the local nuts. The hard-shelled one living upstairs."

The woman was incorrigible, Alex thought. She was also gorgeous. Her vibrant coloring, feminine curves, and shapely legs were set off so dramatically by a slim black skirt, chrome yellow blouse, and black patent pumps, it took all his willpower to grumble instead of hauling her into his arms and kissing her good morning. "Now look, Casey," he forced himself to say as he hung his blazer beside a jacket that was obviously Casey's.

When seeing their clothes side by side stirred him, he decided it was time to do the most mundane thing possible. Making coffee seemed like a good idea. Unfortunately, the coffee maker was on a shelf right behind her. Well, perhaps he could handle that much proximity. To play it safe he kept nagging at her while he forged ahead toward the shelf. "Don't give me technicalities," he scolded. "To all intents and purposes you were alone. If someone decided to vandalize this place and you along with it, I wouldn't do you much good from upstairs. I realize you always have your trusty dictionary, but I'd rest easier if you'd do as I ask and stick to regular hours."

Casey looked over her shoulder at Alex. How cooperative of him, she thought wryly, to give her such a perfect opening. "Why should anyone vandalize *The Weekender*?" she asked.

"Presumably for the same reason an editor would

mess up its copy," he answered, inserting a filter into the basket of the coffee maker.

"And what would that reason be?" she persisted. "Who would be behind that sort of thing?"

Alex was silent for several moments, then shrugged. "Your guess is as good as mine on both counts, Casey. As you said last night, I've made plenty of enemies. I've been taking it more or less for granted that the publisher of *The English Bay Gazette*—my main rival in the weekly market here—is trying to put me out of business and doesn't worry a whole lot about whether he's using ethical tactics to do it. He's something of a thug, probably capable of anything. Then again, maybe I'm being unfair to him. Maybe I'm being an alarmist."

"And maybe you're not," Casey said, deciding to plunge right into the difficult task of telling Alex what she'd heard. She turned to face him, crossed one leg over her other knee, and began nervously tapping the eraser end of a pencil against her palm. "I understand you know Smiley . . ." She realized she had no idea of the diner owner's last name. "Smiley the ex-jockey. At The Starting Gate."

Alex was barely listening as he kept his back to Casey. He was fully occupied with the effort of ignoring the shapely calf and nicely turned ankle perilously close to his hand.

"I left the diner a little while ago," Casey said, then quickly recapped what Smiley had told her, wondering as she spoke whether she was about to see the eruption Brittany had predicted.

To her mild surprise Alex was very quiet, very controlled. "So now somebody has started a rumor to try to undermine my financial credibility with advertisers," he said in low, measured syllables as he finally turned to face her, raking his fingers through his dark hair. "I guess I'm going to have to start taking this dirty-tricks campaign against *The Weekender* more seriously."

Casey wanted to ask Alex whether there was any truth to the rumor, but didn't think it was her place—any more than it was her place to reach up and smooth his rumpled hair or brush the backs of her fingers over the muscle that was working in his jaw. "I'm sorry I didn't put the coffee on," she told him. It was the only thing she could think of to say to make up for having brought him the bad news. "If I'd known you'd be down so early, I'd have been glad to do it."

"What's that? Oh . . . no problem," he said once Casey's apology had sunk in. Despite the serious nature of the report he'd just heard, Alex found himself suppressing a smile. He'd just learned that the smear campaign against his flagship paper had been stepped up, yet his biggest concern at the moment was how to avoid falling victim to the sizzling effects of Casey's incredible legs and the caring softness in her eyes.

He grabbed the coffeepot and headed for the door. Sometimes the best defense, he told himself, was a temporary retreat. "I'll go get some water," he said in a voice so strained, he hardly recognized it as his own. "When I come back, I'll finish making the coffee, then pull up a stool beside you and fill you in on the situation here while we work on the pasteup."

"You will?" Casey said as she swiveled to face her table again. "Fill me in on the situation, I mean?"

Alex gave her a lopsided grin. "I'd better. If I don't, you'll find out on your own." He started through the door, then poked his head back inside the room and winked at her. "Besides, I'm beginning to think I can use an ally, and you seem to fill the bill pretty well."

Well done, he congratulated himself as he made his brief escape. Now all he had to do was to continue to keep things on a friendly but businesslike level until the rest of the staff started arriving. He groaned inwardly. Nobody else was likely to show up until nine. He had to get through nearly two hours of being alone with Casey without giving in to an insane urge to throw caution to the winds and pull her into his arms.

Casey sat staring blankly at the page she'd been working on. A warm languor such as she'd never felt before was moving through her. It was amazing how thrilled she was that Alex seemed ready to offer her a little of his trust.

With a deep sigh she made a private, solemn vow to prove to him that she was worthy of that trust.

For the next two hours Alex gave Casey a great deal to think about, and only a small part of it involved the independent newspaper business.

It was crazy, she thought. There she was with Alex teaching her everything she wanted to know about the nuts and bolts of producing a neighborhood weekly, and it was all she could do to pay attention. She couldn't concentrate fully on the tales Alex related about the rotten stunts he'd been putting up with. How his rival, the owner of *The Gazette*, somehow had the resources to operate at a loss in order to undercut *The Weekender*'s rates; how advertisers were being fed the false information that Alex was giving better rates to their competitors than to them; and most disturbing of all, how they'd printed fake letters to the editor using real people's names, obviously plucked at random from the phone book, which could have gotten *The Weekender* into serious legal trouble except for Alex's long-time policy of checking sources.

For all that Casey was fascinated by what Alex was telling and teaching her, she was constantly distracted by his nearness.

When he was explaining some of the hard facts of weekly newspaper publishing to her, she was dwelling on the low, velvety sound of his voice.

When he was confessing, with remarkable frankness, that even though his company was thriving, he was in hock up to his eyeballs, she was losing herself in the brilliant blue of his eyes.

Everything about Alex excited her. As he expertly put ads in place on the flats, she watched his hands, wondering idly how they would feel caressing her body. When he talked to her, his mouth was tempting almost beyond bearing, his easy grin captivating, and his firm lips inspiring fantasies she'd never known she was capable of conjuring up. Even his scent, a blend of spice and freshly showered male, had to be an aphrodisiac—nothing else could explain its heady effects.

Never in her life had Casey experienced such wild, ungovernable stirrings. A year before, she'd been engaged, yet her fiancé hadn't inspired any of the excitement she was feeling for Alex. Not for a moment had her guard come down with Donald Glenwood. Not once had she allowed herself to be open and vulnerable to him—and only now did it strike her as strange that she'd been able to keep such total control over her responses.

Even when she'd ultimately broken her engagement, on the grounds that Donald was too wrapped up in his glamorous career as a television anchorman to have time to build a strong relationship, she'd been saddened that things hadn't worked out, but certainly not crushed.

Actually, she admitted to herself, she'd been relieved. Donald was a wonderful person, and she'd had enough affection for him to convince herself their marriage would work. But from the moment he'd slipped the ring onto her finger, she'd started having nightmares, breaking out in a cold sweat for no apparent reason, finding fault with the poor man whether he deserved it or not. And she'd *never* been a critical person—well, except perhaps a few times before. Such as whenever any romantic male had threatened to get serious on her.

It had been an act of sheer will that had brought her to the brink of marriage with Donald. She'd decided she had to stop being a fearful child and simply place her trust in a fine man, or she'd never have a family of her own.

But the closer they'd gotten to the wedding date, the more the same old panic had set in. She'd begun to see herself becoming just like her mother and endlessly repeating her own painful childhood, spending the rest of her days in a frantic, hopeless effort to please a man whose demands were impossible to fulfill and whose expectations could never be met. She'd decided she wanted no part of it, and Donald had been gracious when she'd told him she'd had second thoughts. Or grateful, Casey amended wryly. In any event they'd gone back to being fond friends once the awful specter of marriage had been removed.

Alex McLean, she suspected, wasn't as manageable as Donald. Not in any way. Especially not in terms of what he made her feel.

"What does Smiley call you?" Alex asked, startling Casey from her reverie.

She stared at him. "I beg your pardon?"

Alex took a deep breath and let it out slowly, struggling to master his response to the sensual vibrations he was getting from Casey. He wished he knew what was going on behind her expressive eyes—yet he was glad he didn't. He resisted the almost overpowering urge to get involved with her. No matter what he was feeling and wanting, he had to remain aloof. It wouldn't be fair to get tangled up with any woman when his company was demanding all his resources. "I asked," he said carefully, "what Smiley calls you. He gives everyone a nickname. I'm Scoop because I'm in the newspaper business. What does he call you?"

"Strawberry," she answered, her voice husky with desire as she became acutely aware once again of the charged atmosphere around her.

Alex gazed at her wild mane of red gold curls and smiled. "You were tagged with that name for obvious reasons," he said quietly.

She nodded and smiled back at him, wondering why he kept looking at her the way he did without doing anything about it.

"Casey," Alex began, suddenly not sure why he was fighting his intense attraction to her. His mind had gone completely blank on that score. "Casey . . ."

"Yes?" she said eagerly, wishing she had the nerve to throw herself into his arms and see what developed.

A fierce battle raged between Alex's needs and his conscience. His conscience won. "Let me show you an easy way to decide how to stack the ads on an editorial page," he said at last, his tone impersonal.

Casey smiled brightly, pretending to be grateful. And she *was* grateful, she told herself. After all, wasn't she at *The Weekender* for the sole purpose of learning the very things Alex was teaching her?

Wasn't she?

Casey heaved a quiet sigh when the two women who formed the small paper's production department finally bustled in. In their midforties, one plump and maternal, the other wispy thin and timid, Marg Abbott and her little cohort Sandra Taylor brought an aura of down-to-earth reality to a situation that had literally driven Casey to distraction.

"Well, would you look who's back in harness!" Marg said as soon as she saw Alex at the worktable. Her round face was wreathed in a smile.

"And just in time," Sandra added in her small, breathy voice. "It was good of Casey to tell Ron she'd do all those pages by herself, but it's too much for someone who isn't used to it."

Marg chuckled as she switched on her typesetting computer. "Well, Alex, all I can say is that it's refreshing to see you doing some real work again instead of flitting around the country wining and dining big-wheel advertisers."

Alex laughed and kept working.

Some dictator, Casey thought. All of a sudden he was one of the gang. Even Sandra wasn't afraid to speak up to him. Where was the autocrat, the no-arguments-tolerated boss? Why did *she* rate special treatment? Not that he'd been much of a bully this morning, she realized now that she thought about it. He'd been rather sweet, in fact, and endlessly patient no matter how slow she was at putting columns of type in place.

Just before ten Alex stood up, stretched, and yawned.

Casey kept her eyes downcast, trying not to dwell on the narrowness of his waist and the intriguing ripple of muscle she could see through his shirt.

"I think you can handle what's left of the pasteup, Casey," he said, tidying his work area. "I should go to my office and make some phone calls." Leaning down to speak so only she could hear, he added, "For one thing, I want to talk to my bank manager and tell him about Smiley's rumor. If it hasn't reached him yet, I'd prefer he heard it from me. And if he already knows about it, maybe he can help track down where it originated."

Casey couldn't control the involuntary shiver that skittered along her spine as Alex's warm breath caressed the sensitive skin just behind her ear.

"Are you nervous about finishing on your own?" Alex asked, abruptly straightening up. He was getting those vibrations from her again, and he'd come perilously close to brushing his lips over the slender column of her throat.

"I'm not nervous," Casey answered automatically. "I mean, maybe I'm a little . . . anxious. But I can handle the rest of the pasteup. I *want* to handle it. It's the kind of challenge I love."

Alex stood still for a moment, wondering how long he was going to be able to battle Casey's obvious desire as well as his own. Finally he gave her a quick, companionable pat on the shoulder, cleared his throat, and said nonchalantly, "Go to it, Strawberry."

Then he ambled out of the composing room, his hands thrust into his pockets.

And Casey, to her utter dismay, felt bereft when he was gone.

Three

Working his way through his in basket like a one-man assembly line, Alex was setting aside one paper with his left hand while reaching for the next with his right.

He did a double take when he looked at the two-page document he'd picked up. After he'd scanned it, he pushed back his chair, got to his feet, and strode out of his office and across the hall toward the composing room. He felt as if someone had kicked him in the belly, though he wasn't sure why. All he knew was that something wasn't adding up, and that he'd had one too many curves thrown at him since he'd arrived back in Vancouver.

Casey was standing near the composing-room doorway thinking about the hunger pangs that were reminding her it was nearly noon and she'd had nothing more to eat all morning than a muffin. She'd finished doing a last check of the proofreading she'd offered to help Marg with—her own pasteup chores long since completed—when she looked up and saw Alex.

Her heart leapt, and her pulse did a tap dance. Alex had been in his office for two hours, and she'd . . .

She stopped herself from admitting she'd missed him.

Nevertheless, hoping against all common sense that Alex was going to ask her to have lunch with him, she instinctively smiled when he walked into the composing room.

"Casey, I'd like to see you in my office for a minute," he said abruptly. Without waiting for an answer he pivoted on his heel and marched away.

"Sure," Casey answered as she put down the flats and eagerly followed him, wondering what had happened. She hoped his banker or some advertiser hadn't been giving him a hard time. His thunderous expression suggested something even worse. More dirty tricks? Casey was concerned but elated that Alex was going to confide in her again.

"What's up?" she asked as she stepped into what had been, in the mansion's glory days, an enormous dining room. Alex was standing at the bay window facing out, yet Casey could see by his stance that every muscle and nerve was taut, as if he'd reached his breaking point. "What's wrong?" she asked more gently.

Alex turned and gave her a long, searching stare. "You tell me," he finally answered.

She scowled, completely confused. Alex seemed angry. And at *her*! But why? For the past half hour she'd been glowing with pride at having helped get the paper ready on time. Now all of a sudden she felt as if she'd done something terribly wrong.

"What I'd like to know," Alex said, waving the papers he was carrying, "is why the Casey McIntyre of this résumé is working here."

Casey's frown deepened as the truth dawned on

her. Alex wasn't in a confiding mood after all. In fact, he seemed to have gone back to distrusting her. Wonderful, she thought with a surge of righteous anger. It was so good to know that her beyond-the-call-of-duty efforts were appreciated. "What do you mean, the Casey McIntyre of that résumé?" she demanded, her voice dangerously quiet. "Are you suggesting it's phony? Or rather, that I am? Because you can check my references right here and now, and I'll pay the long-distance charges myself."

"I'm sure Ron must have verified your background," Alex answered, belatedly realizing he'd acted too hastily. He wasn't sure what he *was* suggesting, except for one thing: his utter puzzlement. "Just tell me why a person with your credentials would take an assistant editor's job at a rinky-dink tabloid like this," he said, going on the offensive instead of backing down. "Explain that odd situation to me, Casey. Because it doesn't make a whole lot of sense."

"That's an awful thing to say," Casey shot back, momentarily distracted by what Alex had said about his paper. "*The Weekender* is not a rinky-dink tabloid. It's a fine publication. It tackles local issues the big dailies can't be expected to go after. It performs all sorts of community services they can't take care of—"

"You should know," Alex cut in, battling against being softened or sidetracked by Casey's defense of his newspaper. He wasn't sure whether she was sincere or clever, and not knowing was tearing him apart more than he liked to admit. This whole thing was insane. He hardly knew the woman. Why should she matter to him so much? "You've worked both full-time and as a free-lancer at some of the biggest dailies back east," he went on, hating both the cynicism that kept him in doubt about Casey and the vulnerability that made him want so much to believe in her loyalty. "I have a pretty good idea what kind of salary you're making here, Casey. It's peanuts."

Casey put her hands on her hips and glared at him. "It's no such thing. For a neighborhood weekly you pay very well."

"For a neighborhood weekly," Alex repeated, raking his splayed fingers through his hair and wishing it weren't so difficult to keep Casey to the point. She kept going off on a tangent, sticking up for him at the very moment when he was attacking her. "But you don't have to work for any neighborhood weekly," he persisted. "You don't have to work for a newspaper at all. You could go for the really big bucks again, the way you apparently did last year when you signed a government contract as a . . ." He glanced down at the second sheet of her résumé. "A speech-writing and media consultant." He looked up and peered at her as if trying to see something that was hidden from his view. "People don't go from that career level to this without a very good reason, Casey."

"And I happen to have a very good reason," she said evenly. "I explained it to Ron when he interviewed me. It satisfied him, but maybe you'll be less tolerant."

"Try me," Alex suggested, meaning it. He would welcome any explanation at all. Anything that would stop the flood of questions washing through his brain about whether his original suspicions about Casey had been justified, whether he'd misread her responses to him earlier in the morning. He couldn't help wondering if the sensual vibrations he'd sensed from her had actually been edginess because he'd walked in on her when she'd expected him to be asleep upstairs in his apartment. "Just try me," he repeated, hoping his tone didn't sound as pleading to Casey as it did to him.

She slowly wagged her head from side to side and spoke in a defeated tone. "You know, Alex, I've been working my buns off for five hours straight, and I've loved every second of it. But right now I'm tired, hungry, and sorely tempted to suggest what you can do with this job. For both our sakes I'd better toddle off, grab a sandwich and a soothing cup of tea, and then decide whether to fight to win your trust or simply move on to someplace where I won't be suspected of who-knows-what at every turn." She started to leave, convinced that her time at *The Weekender* was over. If she didn't decide to resign— and at this point she fully intended to quit—Alex would probably fire her anyway. She'd just supplied him with a perfectly valid excuse by refusing to answer his question until she'd had her lunch break.

"You're pretty independent," he observed when Casey reached the door.

She paused, looked back over her shoulder, and shot him a defiant smile. "I try to be. It's important to me to be independent. Maybe more important than anything else." Propelling herself forward, she hurried back to the composing room to grab her jacket and leave the building before the tears stinging her eyelids betrayed her by spilling down her cheeks.

The very fact that a weeping jag was a distinct possibility shook Casey to her toes. She'd learned by age six that crying was useless and humiliating, and she'd certainly never indulged in tears on the job. She'd never even come close, though she'd survived battles with some of the meanest, crustiest, toughest curmudgeons in the newspaper business. Such weakness was intolerable, and the way she saw it, Alex McLean was the cause. Therefore, she had to get

Alex McLean out of her life as soon as possible. Period.

Alex, still rooted to the floor in front of the bay window in his office, heard Casey say, "See you later," to Marg and Sandra, click briskly down the hall, open the main door, and gently close it behind her.

He admired her control as he watched her race down the front steps.

All at once it hit him what a stupid thing he'd done. Why had he landed on Casey with both feet over something as ridiculous as her overqualifications? What did he suspect her of? If she'd been planted on his staff to create trouble for him, wouldn't she have shown up with a résumé that seemed reasonable instead of one that gave rise to doubts? And what about his managing editor? Ron Coulter had decided to hire Casey in spite of the questions he must have had about her, and Ron was a hardheaded skeptic of the first order.

And above all, why hadn't he had the grace to thank Casey for making sure the paper was ready on time? Sure, he'd helped, but Casey would have managed without him. She'd have managed if she'd had to work all night.

It would serve him right if he lost her, Alex told himself as he emerged from his trance and tossed the résumé onto his desk. He headed for the composing room, where he shrugged into his blazer, told Marg he'd be out for at least an hour, then charged after Casey.

Catching up with her at the corner two blocks away, Alex grabbed Casey's hand from behind and tugged on it so she'd have to stop.

Startled, she whirled on him with her shoulder bag swinging. She'd have hit him in the face if he hadn't ducked.

"Oh lord, it's *you*!" Casey said, genuinely horrified. The last thing she'd expected was for Alex to follow her. "I thought you were a mugger. I'm sorry!"

"Hey, a belt in the chops with a flying purse would serve me right," Alex said with a fleeting grin that quickly turned into a troubled frown. "I'm the one who's sorry, Casey. Sorry for not telling you how much I appreciate the way you rose to the occasion when a lesser person would have made excuses not to meet our deadline. Sorry for getting off on the wrong foot with you last night. Sorry for playing the heavy because—" He stopped short of admitting it was because she disturbed him in so many ways, on so many levels. Taking her other hand as well, he went on. "Let's just say I was doing my tyrant number for stupid, adolescent reasons. But most of all, Casey, I'm sorry I've become such a cynic that I can't quite accept that someone as terrific as you could have dropped into my life . . ." He cleared his throat. "Could have joined my staff, that is," he amended awkwardly, "with no ulterior motives. I wouldn't blame you for quitting on me, but I wish you wouldn't. I wish you'd forgive me so we could start over."

Casey gave him a faint smile, but didn't answer. It was easy to forgive Alex. Actually, she didn't feel she had anything to forgive him for. He was going through a difficult time, and he was under so much stress, it was no wonder he was having trouble telling the good guys from the bad.

Forgiveness, however, wasn't the issue. Hour by hour, even minute by minute, she was finding out how vulnerable she could be to Alex. She'd never experienced anything like it. She wasn't sure she liked the situation.

And yet . . . she couldn't remember ever feeling

quite as alive as she had since she'd first looked into Alex's intense blue eyes and felt the electricity of his touch. Was she too much of a coward to explore what was happening to her? Was she so afraid of being burned, she was avoiding a lovely warmth?

"Do I sense some hesitance here?" Alex asked. He drew a deep breath and took a chance on appealing both to Casey's humor and her sense of justice. "Dare I point out that it might not be fair for you to resign when the guy who hired you is in a sickbed counting on you to cover for him? Remember, you work for Ron. I'm just the publisher, the temporary interloper getting in the way until Ron gets back and dredges up some excuse to send me out on the road again."

Casey laughed. "Sure, Alex. Just the publisher."

"Have lunch with me," he suggested. "We owe it to Ron to see if we can get through an entire meal without driving each other around the bend."

"Is this an order?" Casey asked teasingly, already aware she was incapable of saying no.

Alex gazed at her for several long moments, then slowly shook his head. "No, Casey. It's not an order. It's an invitation."

"Then I'd love to have lunch with you," she said, adding after a fraction of a beat, "boss."

Alex pretended not to notice that last word, but he felt his jaw unclenching, and an invisible burden was lifted from his shoulders.

Casey had half expected Alex to head for The Starting Gate so he could ask Smiley if he'd heard any more rumors. But she was pleasantly surprised when he suggested a take-out lunch at a Stanley Park picnic table. "The breeze is pretty lively, but otherwise the day's too perfect to waste," he said with almost boyish enthusiasm as they resumed walking. "We can go Mexican, Greek, English fish-and-chips, Italian, or even North American. What do you say?"

"I think a picnic's a great idea, and I'm flexible, foodwise," Casey said with a smile, amazed by the sudden change in Alex. He'd tamped down the Vesuvius inside him so effectively, she wondered if both she and Brittany had overestimated its volatility.

They finally settled on Italian-meatball subs from one of the neighborhood mom-and-pop operations Alex seemed to favor, then cut through the park until they reached a picnic table perched on a high point of land with a panoramic view of the bay and the hazy purple line of mountains on the western horizon.

The spot was idyllic and restful, set far enough away from the busiest sections of the park to allow for privacy. There were a few Frisbee players on the lawn behind them, a ghetto blaster occasionally punctuated the silence for a few seconds, and the grating rasp of roller skates underscored the laughter of passing teenagers. But the park sounds only heightened Casey's awareness of the sudden slowing of time and the aura of utter peacefulness. She began to notice things like the soothing touch of the breeze tickling through her hair and feathering over her skin, the sun's warmth seeping into every fiber of her body, the fragrance of evergreen mingled with summer flowers. Even the savory meatballs and tomato sauce packed into a fresh roll had a special, loving-hands-at-home taste, and the colas Alex had bought to go with the sandwiches seemed to Casey to have more tangy fizz than usual.

Was it the day, she wondered, or the effect of the beautiful park—or was it the company she was keeping that made everything so special? Despite the undercurrents that made conversation with Alex awkward and stilted, she was strangely contented.

Perhaps too contented, she thought, as she finished off her sandwich. Abruptly deciding it was time to break the dangerous spell, she broached the subject of her résumé. "Alex, it's true that I could get a job on a major daily here," she said bluntly. "I turned down an offer right after I arrived. But the very size of the big papers is what puts me off. The impersonal atmosphere. The sense of . . ." She hesitated, then laughed shyly and finished the sentence. "Of not doing anything that actually matters a damn."

"You started out in your journalism career thinking you could change the world," Alex said with a smile. "Then you found out that even the most explosive story made little difference in the grand scheme of things."

Casey beamed at him, realizing that she'd fully expected Alex to understand. And he had. "So I started considering smaller papers that served narrower markets," she continued. "I thought perhaps a journalist could make a difference at that level. But an awful lot of those little papers are essentially shopping guides and advertising vehicles." She paused as she came to the crunch of her story, wondering how Alex was going to react. "To get to the point, I started thinking about how I wanted to use the nest egg I'd built up—I had a small inheritance from my grandmother, some hefty savings from that obscenely fat-cat government contract I sold my soul for last year, and some great investment advice. I decided to go after what I really wanted: my own paper, no matter how tiny, as long as I could make its voice count for something. But I have very little idea how to run a weekly, so I decided I needed on-the-job experience. It was pure luck that landed me in a position to learn from the best in the business."

Alex stared at Casey in disbelief, then tipped back his head and exploded into laughter.

Not sure what was so funny, Casey started to get a little huffy. Did Alex think it was fine for *him* to follow a dream, but not for *her*? Did he think she couldn't handle the challenge? She wished she weren't so mesmerized by the strong cords of his neck. It was difficult to be indignant with the man when she wanted to nibble her way from his collarbone to the little cleft in his chin.

Settling down Alex shook his head and sighed. "How could I have been so blind? Let me give you a quick recap of my résumé, Casey. I was a reporter on a major daily, then a featured columnist, finally an editor. But I started getting the feeling I was another middle manager in a giant corporation that could have been making widgets, for all that its head honchos really cared about newspapers. So I up and quit, then took a low-level job at a weekly so I could learn what I needed to know before starting up my own paper." He laughed again. "Sound familiar? You'd think I'd have recognized the pattern when I saw it, yet when I skimmed through your background, it didn't even cross my mind that you might be doing precisely the same thing I did." Gathering up the debris of their lunch, he began stuffing it into the paper bag it had been packed in. "I'm more than sorry, Casey. I'm appalled. I missed the obvious truth because I was looking for your secret agenda."

As he slid out of his side of the bench and went to toss the garbage into a nearby container, Alex flashed Casey a rueful smile that masked the turmoil he felt. If he'd been shaken back at the office by the discovery of how suspicious he was becoming, he was rocked to his very foundations now. "Are you sure you want to get into this business?" he asked with a laugh. "Look what it's doing to my mentality." Not that the newspaper was entirely to blame, he realized. There were other factors.

Casey smiled and nodded. "I must admit I've been having a few second thoughts since I started at *The Weekender*. Even without somebody out there trying to undermine you, there's constant pressure. And it's scary to know how much can go wrong. How could a person *not* be changed? But Alex, your integrity is still intact. Surely you must feel good about some of the things you've accomplished in the West End. The very fact that you do have enemies says you're making waves."

"I just hope I can keep riding those waves," he commented, glancing at his watch. "There's always the possibility of a wipeout. And I'd better get back to the paper in case some rogue breaker is rolling in on me even as we speak."

"Me too," Casey said, getting to her feet.

Alex frowned at her. "Why? You've done your time this week, and more. Everyone else books off at noon on Fridays. It helps make up for the long hours they put in the rest of the week."

"Do *you* book off at noon?" Casey asked.

Alex saw what was coming, but he argued anyway. "That's different. I own the company. I have to be a slave to it."

"Does Ron book off at noon?" she persisted.

"He's the managing editor. Once we're established enough to give ourselves important-sounding titles, Ron will be a vice president of Pacific Northwest Publications, so he's piling up brownie points while he's at the ground-floor stage."

Casey's eyes sparkled with victory. "Am I not the acting editor while Ron's away?"

"I'm still not sure," Alex said quietly. "Are you, Casey? Are you still with *The Weekender* in spite of its tyrannical, cynical, pain-in-the-neck publisher?"

She moved toward him, touched by the gentle sincerity in his expression. "Yes, if its publisher will still have me . . ." Suddenly one of her heels sank into the lawn, and she stumbled.

With a lightning-quick move, Alex caught her by the shoulders before she fell against him. He swallowed hard as the tips of her breasts brushed against his chest. Her hands curved around his upper arms so she could steady herself, and she looked up at him, her eyes dark and luminous. The flaring heat of her gaze ignited white-hot fires inside him. His throat constricted until he couldn't have spoken if he'd tried. And he didn't try, because he was incapable of lucid thought. Casey's unique, elusive fragrance was intoxicating him, and her mouth was demanding his attention, all that full pink softness luring him closer and closer, until his lips were almost grazing hers. . . .

But his infernal conscience got in the way and hit him like a cold splash of water. He had no right to indulge in sensual games with Casey. He had nothing to offer her except what she'd signed on for—an apprenticeship in the business of running a neighborhood weekly. "Hey," he said with a stilted grin as he forced himself to draw back from her and drop his hands to his sides, "I just thought of something, Casey McIntyre. If you're working for *The Weekender* in order to prepare for operating your own paper, I'm training a potential competitor."

"Not on your life," Casey assured him, going along with the pretense that Alex hadn't been on the verge of kissing her. Her lips were tingling again, and her heart was dancing to a primitive rhythm, but she acted out her part. "I'd never be foolish enough to go head-to-head against an Alex McLean publication," she went on with an amazing semblance of normality, considering that she was toying with the idea of wrapping her arms around the man's neck and *taking* the kiss she was beginning to feel he owed her.

"Where would you do it?" he asked distractedly. Reining in his feelings seemed to be getting more difficult with every moment he spent in Casey's company. He was getting vibrations again. Strong ones. Dangerous ones.

Temporarily losing interest in the question he'd asked, he cupped his fingers under Casey's elbow to propel her toward the pavement. The park was treacherous, he'd decided. Funny how he'd never noticed its enchanted-forest allure until now. Funnier still how he felt as if he'd never noticed much of anything until now. Had he spent the first thirty-four years of his life in a state of semiconsciousness? A kind of limbo? Had some evil wizard put a curse on him when he'd been born that could be broken only by the kiss of a Princess Charming?

Alex found his lips twitching with amusement as he realized how far gone he was.

Carefully picking her way across the lawn Casey slanted him a puzzled look, then raced along beside him on the paved roadway, feeling slightly put out when he let go of her elbow and thrust his hands into his pockets. She wanted to carry on with her side of their conversation so Alex wouldn't know how addled he'd made her, but she couldn't remember what she'd said before he'd asked her where she'd do it—whatever "it" was. Her imagination had had a field day with any number of possibilities. "Where would I do what?" she asked at last.

Alex's forehead creased in a confused frown, and he recalled that he'd asked Casey something. He finally came up with it. "Where would you start up? Your paper, I mean."

"In a small town somewhere," Casey answered, sighing inwardly. All of a sudden Alex wanted to talk shop. Well, why not? Apparently nothing more interesting was about to happen. "I wouldn't try to get established anywhere near here, of course," she went on as crisply as she could. "You have this market pretty well covered. I do find I love the ocean, so I've been considering someplace on the east coast. Nova Scotia, maybe."

"Nova Scotia?" Alex repeated in a slightly strangled voice. A whole continent away! All his stomach muscles knotted up again, and bleakness washed over him. "Nova Scotia's probably a good choice," he said as soon as he could get hold of himself, but then added hastily, "There are still lots of openings in this area, though. I operate in a few Vancouver suburbs and outlying areas, a couple of villages up the coast, and just one town in the interior. I was kidding about training a competitor, Casey. There's always room for a healthy rivalry." After a few seconds he asked tentatively, "Have you any idea when you'll make your move?"

"I have a lot to learn before I come to any decision," Casey answered, wondering if she'd imagined the urgency in Alex's voice, as if he didn't want her to go far away. But it was probably wishful thinking, she told herself. If he wouldn't let down his guard for a stolen kiss or two—and she supposed she should be glad he wouldn't—why would he care where she went to set herself up in business?

"I spent a full year at the weekly where I served my

apprenticeship," Alex saw fit to point out after a troubled silence.

"I imagine it would take at least a year to soak up everything there is to know," Casey agreed eagerly. "It's a big financial risk, so I'd want to have a really solid grounding in every phase of the operation. You're sure you don't feel I'm using you?"

Use me! Alex urged silently. *Use me any way you like!* "On the contrary," he said aloud. "To have someone of your caliber on my side is like being handed a secret weapon, Casey. And anyway, how could I fault you for something I did myself? I was up front about it with the weekly publisher who hired me, so it seemed like a fair deal. It still does, even now that I'm on the other side of the bargaining table." He wasn't being entirely truthful, he admitted to himself. To have Casey around long enough to get used to seeing her, talking to her, absorbing the effects of her femininity, only to wave good-bye to her after she'd really gotten under his skin? What was fair about a deal like that?

Casey was quiet, too busy glowing from Alex's "secret weapon" comment to talk about her future as a publisher.

"Actually, you'll probably have an easier time launching a weekly than I did," Alex remarked. "I had to deal with at least one difficulty you're not likely to face."

"Oh? What's that?" Casey asked with mild curiosity.

"A wife who thought that quitting a great job to take a flyer on something as anachronistic as a crusading weekly newspaper would be the height of irresponsibility, not to mention rank stupidity."

Casey's heart stopped dancing. Stopped, period. Yet somehow she kept walking, rubbery knees and all.

At least now, she told herself, she understood why Alex kept pulling back, just short of kissing her.

Four

"I imagine your wife must realize by now that starting your own chain of newspapers wasn't so irre-
sponsible after all," Casey managed to say, even
though she was reeling from Alex's offhand remark.
And she *was* reeling, like a prizefighter struggling up
from the mat after taking a sucker punch. How could
she have overlooked the possibility that Alex was
married? She was thirty years old, a veteran of the
singles' scene.

Yet with Alex, Casey realized, she'd been as naive
and unsuspecting as a teenager. Why?

Noticing that he was giving her a quizzical look as
he strolled along in blissful ignorance of the blow
he'd dealt her, Casey realized her foolish distress was
showing. "After all," she continued, determined to
maintain her dignity even if her brains seemed to
have taken a dive, "even if you're having a few little
problems right now, there's no doubt that you're a
success."

A definite catch in Casey's voice confirmed Alex's
suspicion that he'd seen a stricken expression in her

eyes, and the determined set to her jaw revealed, by a strange paradox, an unexpected fragility. He regretted the impression he'd given her with his careless remark about his wife. He'd forgotten that Casey probably didn't know about his divorce, even though most of Vancouver seemed to have been privy to all the gory details when his marriage had finally self-destructed. "I have no idea what my ex-wife thinks now," he said, unable to suppress a tiny smile. Casey was upset to think he was married. He shouldn't be pleased, but he couldn't help it. "JoBeth's remarried and living in California."

Mingled relief and consternation suffused Casey's features. "Your marriage broke up because you wanted to start your own paper?"

"Not at all. It broke up because it never should have existed in the first place. It was a matter of mistaken identity. Each of us saw what we wanted to see in the other, not what was really there. And to be honest, it turned out I was lousy husband material, for any number of reasons. I tend to think and act as an individual, not as half of a couple."

Casey laughed softly. "I know exactly what you mean."

Alex looked sharply at her. "You've been involved with that kind of person?"

"No, I've *been* that kind of person. Still am. I was luckier than you, though. I realized the error of my ways before I headed for the altar." She told him briefly about her ill-fated engagement to Donald Glenwood, then sighed. "I don't know, Alex, maybe this problem of independence and thinking as an individual is an occupational hazard. I'll bet one of the bones of contention with your wife was that you'd go chasing after a story that could involve danger—or at least being late for dinner—and she thought perhaps you should pause for reflection on the possible consequences."

It was Alex's turn to laugh. Casey had zeroed in with such accuracy, she made him realize what a textbook case the breakdown of his marriage probably was. "Work always has seemed to take up the number-one spot in my life," he admitted. "And let's face it—a woman has a right to be at the top of her husband's priority list." He paused, wondering why he was dwelling so long on this subject. It wasn't one he normally chose to talk about. "Anyway," he continued, deciding to wrap it up, "all I meant a minute ago was that I'd have started my own paper long before I did, but JoBeth was dead set against it. I didn't go ahead until the divorce settlement had been worked out." And then not for quite some time, he added silently. Financially he'd had to start all over from ground zero.

Catching a contradiction in what Alex was saying, Casey opened her mouth to mention that a man who relegated his own ambitions to the back burner for his wife's sake didn't seem to have put his work ahead of his marriage. But it occurred to her that she was all too ready to leap to Alex's defense. It also dawned on her that she couldn't blame Alex's marital state for his failure to take her into his arms. "All I can say is that I'm glad you finally did launch your weeklies," she murmured thoughtfully, deciding she must have been imagining the electricity she'd been feeling from Alex. Obviously the excitement she'd sensed between them was one-sided. No wonder he wanted to stick to shop talk. The starry-eyed gazes she kept beaming his way probably embarrassed him. Now they were embarrassing her.

Searching desperately for an impersonal topic of conversation, Casey looked around, then blessed her sheer good luck. "Isn't that the famous cedar?" she said brightly, pointing toward a huge tree on one corner. "The one you saved from the developer?"

"That's the cedar all right, but I didn't save it," Alex answered. "Concerned citizens did. And it wasn't just a save-a-tree party. It was a general protest against the developer in question and the officials who've been letting him ride roughshod over local building regulations."

"Dawson Developments?" Casey asked. "The company you claim needs investigating, along with the bureaucrats Dawson has been dealing with and quite possibly bribing?"

Alex gave her a smile and nodded. "You really have done your homework, Casey. Our last run at Dawson was well over a month ago, probably before you even arrived in Vancouver."

Casey shrugged. Doing her homework was nothing special. It was part of the job. "I got here in time to read about the demonstrations in all the local papers, and my curiosity sent me digging through back copies of *The Weekender*. I found a series of editorials that I'm sure were responsible for whipping up public interest." She stopped dead as a thought struck her. "Who wrote those pieces?"

"I did," Alex answered, then grinned. "You assumed it was Ron. It wouldn't have occurred to you that the publisher might be responsible."

"Okay, I admit it. But that was before I found out that Alex McLean is a hands-on publisher."

Or would like to be, Alex couldn't help thinking as he fought to keep his hands in his pockets instead of reaching out to cradle Casey's upturned face between his palms and savor her tempting mouth.

They reached the construction site and stopped to watch the progress of the building project for a moment or two. "I think you can count the Dawson company among those enemies of yours," Casey remarked, then shook her head as she recalled how hard-hitting Alex's editorials had been. "In fact, I'm amazed your kneecaps are still intact."

"If I wasted time worrying about my kneecaps, I'd have to go into another business." Alex scowled as he realized he and Casey were standing around watching a work crew that probably had no particular fondness for him. "We'd better move along," he suggested, cupping his hand under Casey's elbow.

But he was too late. At that very moment a deep voice from the construction site boomed. "Well, look who's come to visit his pet tree."

Alex followed the direction of the voice and saw the foreman of the crew standing by a table piled with blueprints. The man's name was Vic Lundstrom, Alex remembered. Big, brawny, and grizzly-bear mean, Vic didn't look any friendlier right now than he had the last time Alex had seen him, on the day the public outcry against the Dawson bulldozers had brought the project to a temporary standstill.

Alex stood his ground as Vic placed a large rock on the blueprints to hold them down, then sauntered toward him.

"Who's the Paul Bunyan clone?" Casey quietly asked Alex, adrenaline instantly pumping through her.

Alex cursed himself under his breath for having walked into this kind of stupid confrontation when Casey was with him. He should have realized Lundstrom would hold a grudge. "I'd like you to go home now, or at least head back to the office," he said to Casey instead of answering her. There was no way he would back down from Lundstrom, but he didn't want Casey anywhere nearby if things got out of hand. "I'll catch up in a minute," he assured her.

"Why? What's going to happen?" she asked, scowling as two more hulks formed a rear guard behind the first one. "I don't think these walking mountains are forming a committee to give you an award for your contribution to environmental awareness, Alex."

He was inclined to agree. "I said *go*," he ground out through clenched teeth. "*Now*, Casey! Move it!"

When Casey saw yet another hard hat fall in as if joining a gathering army, she decided that she should take Alex's advice—in part. She backed away from him.

"McLean, what do you want around here?" Lundstrom asked as he came to a stop a few feet from Alex, his feet planted wide apart and his thumbs hooked into his belt. "You planning to make more trouble? You already did a pretty good number on us, buddy. You slowed us down, but good."

"What's your problem, Vic?" Alex asked calmly. "You and your men get paid by the hour. Why should you worry if doing the job properly means taking a little longer?"

"You ever hear of bonuses for finishing ahead of schedule? You cost us, and if there's a slowdown in all the Dawson projects, you'll cost us a whole lot more, buddy boy."

"That's unfortunate, *pal*," Alex said with a deliberately sarcastic inflection, "but as long as Jimmy Dawson keeps trying to make his millions by playing fast and loose with this city's building codes—among other things—I'll do my best to keep right on costing you. Maybe you and your crew ought to consider applying for jobs with decent developers. Have you done one single project for Dawson that you're proud of? How long are you going to keep taking your orders from a sleaze?"

The foreman's eyes blazed with sudden rage. Alex's words had hit home, and hit hard. "Lemme tell you about Jimmy's orders," Vic snarled. "Jimmy says he doesn't want you near any of his properties. He says if you show your face around here, I should maybe rearrange it for you. I'm beginning to like the idea."

Alex wished he could tell whether Casey had made tracks. He couldn't afford to check on her right at the moment, because he had to try to stare these men down. "You and all your little friends?" he drawled, hoping sheer bravado would discourage any rough stuff Vic and his men were mulling over.

"Yeah. Me and all my little friends," Lundstrom answered.

Bravado didn't always work, Alex realized as all four men slowly moved in on him, grinning as if they were relishing a little bone-crunching exercise in the middle of the day. He was trying to stay cool on the outside, but inside he was boiling mad, and more than ready to start swinging. He hoped Casey was well out of . . .

"Yoo-hoo, fellas," a singsong, ultrafeminine voice cooed.

Alex, along with all the other men, turned to gape at the ditsy female who was idiotic enough to interrupt the start of a serious rumble. His heart lurched. Casey had edged her way over to the blueprint table and was touching the rock paperweight with her fingertips, stroking it as if she were Zsa Zsa coveting the biggest diamond in captivity. She was smiling sweetly and looking as enchanting as a wood nymph, the breeze whipping her blond curls every which way. What was she up to?

"Get outta here, lady," Lundstrom growled, though

there was a gleam of male interest in his narrowed eyes.

"But I wanted to ask about this paperweight you're using," Casey simpered in a perfect Marilyn Monroe imitation. "It's so unusual. So big and craggy and . . . and so *heavy*!" With another dazzling smile she picked up the rock and stepped away from the table.

"Hey!" Vic shouted. "Put that back, you dizzy broad!"

"Oh dear, I'm sorry!" Casey cried as the breeze caught the blueprints, carried them off the table, and sent them rolling across the property in all directions. "Oh my goodness, look what's happening to your squiggly pictures. I hope they're not important or anything!"

Alex winced at the volley of curses and dire threats that filled the air as the hard hats forgot him and raced off on a paper chase.

Casey hurried back to him, grinning with satisfaction. "You'd better get me out of here, boss. I think those men might be a teeny bit cranky by the time they've finished retrieving their precious blueprints."

"You think *they're* cranky?" Alex said as he grabbed her hand and started moving on the double. "Baby, wait'll you hear from *me*!"

By the time they were climbing the creaking front steps at *The Weekender* building, Alex had already subjected Casey to an on-the-run lecture: She was a naive easterner who'd stuck her pretty nose into something she didn't understand. He wasn't in the habit of being rescued from a tight spot by a woman, and he thanked her very much, but he would thank her a whole lot more just to do what she was told from now on. He didn't know where his mind had been to let her be drawn into a volatile situation that was none of her concern.

Casey hadn't managed to get a word in edgewise, but she hadn't tried very hard. She'd been too absorbed in the drama of Alex's inexplicable fury. Besides, she thought it was good for him to rant and rave a bit. He was a human pressure cooker, and he needed to let off some steam.

Alex cursed quietly but colorfully when he opened the main door and heard the whine of a floor-scrubbing machine. He'd forgotten about the Friday-afternoon office cleaners. But dammit, he wasn't through with his assistant editor yet! He headed for the stairway at the end of the hall, with Casey still in tow. There was one place he could count on for privacy.

Casey realized they were on their way up to his apartment. She was curious about where he lived. She wondered how much more scolding he planned to subject her to, but she was too fascinated by the whole turn of events to be overly concerned.

Alex hauled her to the middle of his living room, stopped, then grabbed her shoulders to whirl her around to face him. She got a general impression of furniture that could be termed eclectic. It was the standard tweed couch, brown corduroy armchairs, walnut veneer end tables, and functional lamps that newly created ex-husbands tended to buy during a grudging sweep through a furniture warehouse. Casey strongly suspected that Alex had been burned in more ways than one when his marriage had broken up. Then again, maybe she was taking his side as usual, with no evidence to go on. She certainly seemed to be prejudiced in his favor, considering she hardly knew the man—and considering that he was scowling and working his jaw as if he were about to take a bite out of her. Not a friendly nibble, either. She decided to try heading him off. Enough, after all, was enough. "Vic and the boys didn't chase us," she said cheerfully.

"I didn't think they would," Alex snapped out. "Those goons were flexing a little muscle because I happened to have been distracted enough to stand around gawking at them, but they weren't about to leave the site and tear through the West End after us."

"Then why the big hurry?" she asked resisting the urge to ask Alex just what had been distracting him. "And why do you keep yelling at me?"

"I'm not yelling at you," he said very quietly. "I haven't raised my voice once."

"Maybe not, but it sounds like yelling to me. Anyway, aren't you overreacting a little?"

Alex frowned, suspecting Casey was right. His behavior appalled him, yet he couldn't seem to simmer down. "Casey, don't you have any idea what you did back there?" he finally asked, trying very hard to strike a calm, reasoned note. "Doesn't it occur to you that Vic Lundstrom's probably planning right now to break your pretty neck the next time he sets eyes on you?"

"Of course it occurs to me," she said patiently. Casey was tempted to point out that so far during his tirade Alex had referred to her pretty nose and her pretty neck, and that she thanked him for the flattering inventory—but she decided he might not see the humor in her remark. Time to go on the offensive. "I'm not stupid, you know. But if you honestly expected me to run for cover when you were about to become human hamburger, you've been hanging around with a sissy crowd. Like it or not, boss, I'm in on this caper. . . ." Casey paused, then added with a puzzled scowl, "Whatever it is, exactly."

"*Caper!*" Alex exploded. "You think making a fool of a foul-tempered construction foreman in front of his men is a *caper*? You think getting involved in crossing the likes of Jimmy Dawson is a *caper*? That guy's not playing games, Casey!"

"He most certainly is!" she shot back. "He's playing silly, school-yard, king-of-the-castle games, complete with bullies. And so what? Name anything—business, politics, law, even most friendships you see these days—everything's a game. And I happen to get a kick out of playing in the macho league. The opponents are so predictable."

"Everything is not a game," Alex said evenly, getting his temper back under control. "Being beaten to a pulp by four macho, predictable goons isn't, for instance."

"Oh, I don't know," Casey drawled. "Look at Monday-night football. Anyway, you're the one who took on Dawson in the first place. And I didn't see you backing down from his gorillas."

"That's different. Jimmy Dawson's a blight on this city. Vancouver's not a temporary stop for me. It's the place I grew up in, the one I plan to stay in. Running Dawson out of town is my problem, not yours. My fight, not your fight. Those gorillas are mine to deal with—you keep your distance. And *that's* an order."

Casey stubbornly shook her head. "Sorry, boss. As long as I'm part of your team, your problems are my problems, your fights are my fights, and your gorillas are my gorillas."

Alex's expression turned to menacing as he stared at her in dumbfounded silence, and for some reason Casey couldn't comprehend, she found herself goading him, almost as if to see if she could *make* him blow his top. "Hey boss," she said with a devilish grin, "you're beautiful when you're mad, you know that?"

He still didn't say a word. He just kept looking at her, his gaze so searching and penetrating, Casey was mesmerized. She held her breath. She could almost hear volcanic rumbles coming from somewhere deep inside the man. The irrepressible excitement she was feeling mounted with every passing second. She wondered whether she'd pushed Alex over the brink. Crazily, she hoped so.

To her wide-eyed amazement he suddenly burst into uproarious laughter and pulled her hard against him, wrapping his arms around her and holding her so close, she could hardly breathe. She didn't care. Breathing wasn't important. If this was Alex's explosion, she was glad she'd nudged him along.

"What am I going to do with you?" he murmured when his laughter subsided. "Should I fire you for your own good?"

Casey tipped her head back and smiled up at him. "If you do, I'll go after the Dawson story as a freelancer. There seems to be more to it than I'd realized, and I'm intrigued."

"So if I want to prevent you from taking on the likes of Lundstrom by yourself, I have to keep you on my team, where I have some control over you?"

"That's about the size of it," she said sweetly.

Alex sighed in defeat. "You drive a hard bargain, Strawberry." He studied her for another long moment that sent a tremor through her, then said softly, "Life has some wild twists, doesn't it? Yesterday at this time I didn't know you existed. Today . . ." He shook his head in utter bemusement before going on in a husky whisper. "My problems are your problems, my fights your fights . . ." He brushed his lips over her forehead, her temples, her brows. "And my gorillas your gorillas," he murmured with a gentle smile. "Not quite the Song of Ruth, but it's the nicest thing anybody's ever said to me."

Turning her head so her mouth would meet his, Casey reached up to plunge her fingers into the dark sable of his hair. Tentative at first, the kiss gradually deepened to a tender mutual demand. Alex's lips were warm and firm as they moved over Casey's. Hers were soft and surrendering, and when he teased at them with his tongue, they parted to invite deeper, more intimate forays.

Casey's senses leapt in response to the incredible new universe of pleasure opening up to her. The taste of Alex was as heady as rare, musky wine, spiced by the bouquet of his delicious male scent. His hands radiated heat and strength as they moved over her back, shaping her pliant curves until she was molded perfectly to his rigid contours. When he flattened his palm over the base of her spine, pressing her against him so she could feel his throbbing need, every part of her being turned to molten quicksilver. Her heartbeat thundered in her ears like a pounding surf, but she heard Alex's low groan as he feasted on her mouth. Instinctively she moved her hips against him and felt every sinew of his body tighten as another groan tore from his throat. Continuing to hold her against him with one hand, he brought the other up to caress her cheek with his fingertips, then smoothed his palm over the column of her throat. When Casey arched her back and murmured incoherently, Alex began undoing the buttons of her blouse, gradually parting the silky material until her lace-covered breast filled his palm.

The aching tenderness of his kisses became a fierce demand as Alex kneaded first one soft mound, then the other, his thumb and forefinger teasing the engorged nipples that thrust against the filigreed cloth.

Casey was gasping with mingled need and pleasure, shimmers of delight rippling through her. But when Alex blazed searing kisses over her throat and the upper slope of her breast, then pushed the lace aside, cupped the quivering fullness in his palm, and finally bent to take the swollen pink tip into his mouth, she cried out softly and felt tears of sheer, raw emotion slip from the corners of her eyes to slide down her cheeks. She was on fire, as if she'd fallen into the very heart of a volcano. Nothing like it had ever happened to her before. She hadn't believed herself capable of such intense feeling. "Alex, it's too much," she said raggedly. "Too much . . . or not enough. . . . Oh lord, I don't know what's happening. . . . Please . . ."

Exulting in Casey's uninhibited passion, Alex was retracing his path, grazing his lips and tongue over her flushed throat toward her mouth, when he tasted the salt of her tears. Shocked, he pulled back and straightened up. He closed his eyes and took a deep breath, expelling it on a slow, measured count as he struggled for self-control. When he could trust himself again, he tugged the lace of Casey's bra back into place and began refastening the buttons of her blouse.

Casey stared at him through glazed eyes, dropping her hands to her sides.

"Of all the selfish, idiotic stunts I've ever pulled in my life," he said in a raspy voice, his features suddenly hard, "this takes the cake." When Casey's blouse was done up, he cradled her face in his hands and brushed away her tears with the sides of his thumbs. "I'm going to take you home now," he said quietly.

Casey knew he was misinterpreting her reaction. "You don't understand," she told him with an urgency that astonished her. "I didn't want you to stop, Alex. I was just so . . . so overwhelmed."

"I know, Casey," he said, his expression pained. "And that's the reason I backed off."

She frowned, totally confused. He'd called a halt *because* of her response? "Oh," she said as his meaning finally got through to her. A self-respecting male didn't play with women who took these things too seriously. And Alex was a self-respecting male. He didn't want to hurt her. Well, that was very kind of him, she told herself, twisting away from him and immediately glancing around for her purse. At some point—she wasn't sure when—she'd tossed it aside. Spying the handbag on a nearby chair, she went to retrieve it. "I don't want you to take me home, Alex, and this time I insist," she said as firmly as she could manage.

Alex started to protest, but Casey held up her hand in a stop gesture. "If you're worried about Vic and the boys, don't. The project site isn't on my way, and the streets I'll be on will be overflowing with people at this hour." She managed a tiny smile as she headed for the door. "And to be honest, right now I really could use some time alone. As I'm sure you've noticed, these past few minutes have shaken me up a little."

"I understand," Alex said, hating himself for the hurt he was seeing in Casey's eyes. Why had he let things go so far? "See you on Monday?" he added lamely when she was halfway out the door.

"Of course," Casey answered, keeping her smile pasted on. She was determined to preserve whatever pride she could. "I won't be spending all that much time in the office, though. I'll be out doing interviews and looking for story ideas. I do most of my writing on my laptop at home, so unless Ron's flu lasts a while, I'll hardly show my face around here at all. I'm more of a roving reporter than an editor."

Alex forced a smile in return. "Just don't rove into trouble, okay?"

"Don't worry about me, boss," Casey answered with a lift of her chin. "I've been taking care of myself for a long time, in all sorts of situations." Except, she added silently as she shut the door and hurried down the stairs, this sort of situation. Thanks to her inexperience with such powerful emotions, she'd made a complete fool of herself.

Rooted to the spot Alex stared at the closed door as he battled the urge to go after Casey.

He was shaking, his hands clenched into tight fists he almost wished he could use on himself. There was no excuse for what he'd done. Sure, he'd been deeply moved by her offbeat your-gorillas-are-my-gorillas declaration. Yes, he'd responded to Casey's desire as much as to his own acute hunger for her. And certainly it was easy to rationalize that she was thirty years old and didn't need him to shield her from the sparks flying between them.

But Casey was a thirty-year-old innocent, whatever her experience with men might be. Alex knew without the slightest doubt that she was a cautious woman who'd been caught off guard by the strength of her emotions, a woman who wouldn't give herself easily, but when she did—as she had with him—it would be completely, generously, and without reservation.

He remembered a time when he'd been that open

and trusting, when he'd had a well of honest passion as deep as Casey's to dip into, when he'd believed . . .

He reached up and passed a hand over his eyes, suddenly feeling very tired, and wishing there were some way he could peel off the protective layers he'd wrapped around himself over the years.

Somewhere inside his self-created cocoon was the Alex McLean who might have deserved what Casey had to offer.

Five

Casey stopped in at her apartment only long enough to change to sneakers, jeans, and a comfortable T-shirt. A long stroll was in order. She needed to clear her brain.

She'd circled the entire perimeter of the Stanley Park peninsula before she'd calmed down enough to think rationally and accept the simple possibility that Alex, while no longer married, might well be involved with someone else, or might not want to get tangled up with anyone. Either way she was lucky he was too decent to lead her on. The self-preserving instincts that had served her so well in the past seemed to have deserted her where Alex was concerned. Why did he strike such a responsive chord in her?

Lost in thought Casey was almost surprised to find herself approaching The Starting Gate. A handwritten sign taped to the diner's window stopped her in her tracks: Smiley was pushing Ruby's famous deep-dish apple pie as a Friday-afternoon special.

Casey laughed, recalling Smiley's comments that the gossipy junior accountants from a few days before had loved that pie. Was he trying to lure them back? She wouldn't put it past him. Scoop inspired that kind of loyalty. She should know.

She went inside, slid onto the last vacant stool at the counter, and grinned at Smiley. "I can't stay away," she said when he raised an eyebrow and glanced at the overhead clock, obviously surprised to see her in the early afternoon. "This diner's becoming my second home."

"What'll it be?" he asked as he worked with lightning-quick motions, flipping burgers on the grill and preparing buns with the various trimmings. "Late lunch or early coffee break?"

"Early coffee, but I'm not in a big hurry," Casey answered, glad Smiley was doing his usual roaring business but wishing the diner weren't quite so crowded. She wanted to ask him whether the apple-pie ploy had worked.

Moving over to her a few minutes later with a steaming mug of freshly made coffee, Smiley leaned close as he set down the cup, pushed back his jaunty jockey's cap, and said quietly, "Stick around awhile, Strawberry. No telling who might show up. It's getting close to that time of day."

Casey's eyes danced. She'd always loved playing spy. And she really was burning to find out where the rumor about Alex's newspaper had started. Maybe then it could be stopped. "You know, I believe I will stay for a bit," she decided aloud. "There's a crossword puzzle in my purse that I've been dying to get at, and I might even sample some of Ruby's famous apple pie a little later on."

"I'll give you the high sign if I spot anybody you oughta meet," Smiley said out of the side of his mouth, then straightened up and went back to his grill, whistling nonchalantly.

Casey had to suppress a giggle. Smiley might make a very good secret agent, she mused. Nobody would believe he was the real thing.

Lunch customers came and went, and after a while Vancouver's notorious start-the-weekend-early crowd began trickling in. By her fourth coffee refill, Casey was giving up on the remote possibility that her quarry would show up, but she didn't have the heart to tell Smiley.

She was staring off into space, trying to wrestle the diabolical creator of *The New York Times* crossword to the mat, when she suddenly noticed Smiley sending her some agitated eye signals. Following the direction of his sidewise glance, she saw a gangly young man in a business suit lowering himself onto a stool two places away from her. "I'll have the deep-dish apple pie," he said in an important-announcement tone.

As Smiley delivered the order, Casey studied the newcomer dubiously. Was this child supposed to be one of the two accountants who'd been talking about the supposed demise of *The Weekender*? He hardly looked old enough to have control of his own piggy bank! She must have misunderstood Smiley's message.

When Smiley turned to her with a questioning lift of his brows, she frowned and gave her head a tiny shake to let him know she had no idea what he was trying to tell her.

He rolled his eyes, then looked down at the fresh-faced youth and nodded determinedly.

With a shrug Casey decided to test the waters. "Does anybody around here know a seven-letter word for a financial loss?" she asked. She already knew the answer, but she'd saved the clue just in case she had occasion to engage some fiscal boy wonder in conversation.

Out of the corner of her eye Casey saw Junior's forehead crease from the effort of hard thinking.

There was a long silence. Then Smiley looked up with a triumphant smile. *"Deficit!"* he exploded.

Casey's head snapped up, and she stared at him in frustration.

Smiley winced, realizing he'd spoiled Casey's plan.

With a forgiving smile Casey looked down at her puzzle again. Fortunately she'd earmarked several suitable clues.

The very next one worked, to her relief. She was beginning to feel silly.

"Could I have a look at that?" Junior said, moving to the stool next to Casey and flashing a smile he obviously considered irresistible.

Gotcha, Casey thought with a surreptitious grin at Smiley.

Now all she had to do was find out where the young man—or his absent cohort—had come by that baseless rumor.

Alex was already awake when Saturday dawned. He'd slept fitfully, despite the exhaustion that seemed to be his constant companion lately. He was dealing with too much work, too much worry, too much everything—and most of all, too much hunger for a certain strawberry blond who'd invaded his thoughts and dreams. With a wry smile he tiredly climbed out of bed and headed for the shower.

After downing a couple of toasted frozen waffles and enough strong coffee to jolt him into some semblance of alertness, Alex dressed in white ducks and a navy T-shirt, then went downstairs to his office to study the intricacies of some new tax regulations that affected his business.

By the time he'd worked his way through that paperwork, it was after ten—a good time, he decided, to go out and visit some of his regular retail advertisers. Nowadays he had salesmen to service the accounts, but a little customer-relations backup from the publisher never hurt.

The day had already offered up a typical Vancouver smorgasbord of weather—sunny one minute, overcast the next. Alex went back upstairs to pull on a lightweight yellow slicker before starting out on his rounds.

Hours later, at the beginning of a light shower that would undoubtedly pass within a few minutes, Alex found himself pushing open the door of The Starting Gate, his glance flickering swiftly over the customers at the diner's long counter. Only when a vague disappointment settled over his spirit like the gray mist shrouding the mountains did he realize he'd been hoping Casey might be there for a late lunch.

All at once it dawned on him that he'd been on edge throughout his whole morning's wanderings, tensing every time he glimpsed a woman who bore even the slightest resemblance to Casey.

Alex McLean, he told himself with weary resignation, *you've got it bad.*

Smiley wasn't around. His wife was taking a turn behind the counter. A full-blown redhead at least a head taller than her husband, Smiley's adored and adoring Ruby had lips and nails that lived up to her name—her real one, which Smiley evidently liked too much to change to a nickname—and a wardrobe of flamboyantly bright slacks and tops styled like jockeys' silks.

"Hi Scoop, honey," Ruby said cheerfully as Alex

took a seat at the counter. "What'll it be? If you're looking for lunch, I've still got some soup left, guaranteed to cure whatever ails you. Healthy too. My sweetie says I outdid myself on this one."

Alex grinned. "Sounds perfect, Ruby. Where *is* your sweetie, by the way? Assuming you mean Smiley, that is."

Ruby hooted with laughter, as if Alex had said the funniest thing she'd ever heard. When she settled down, she dished up his soup and cut an extra-thick slab of bread for him. "As if I'd ever look at any other guy," she said, chuckling as she set the hearty lunch on the counter. "Listen, when you've got a thoroughbred like my Smiley at the post, you don't go placing bets on also-rans."

"No, I guess you don't." Alex said, his thoughts instantly going to a particular thoroughbred he'd like to . . .

"Anyhow, I sent the hubby home for a siesta," Ruby said, cutting into his brief but vivid daydream.

Alex took a deep breath and let it out slowly as he cleared his mind of visions he shouldn't be allowing in the first place. Once he was in control of himself again, he tasted the soup, paused to deliver the rave review he knew Ruby was waiting for, then asked when Smiley would be back. "I wanted to ask him about something," he explained, dipping his spoon into the soup again before Ruby asked him if there was something wrong with it.

"Well, if it's about what I think it is," Ruby said in a low, confidential tone, "I understand Strawberry has everything under control."

Alex froze, the spoon suspended halfway to his mouth.

"You don't like your soup?" Ruby asked with a scowl.

Coming to, Alex struggled through the rest of his meal, though his appetite had abruptly disappeared. He kept telling himself that Ruby's cryptic comment didn't have to mean that Casey was off getting herself into some kind of trouble, but he couldn't think of anything else it *could* mean.

There weren't many people left in the diner by the time Alex was ready to leave, and no one was sitting close to him, so when he was paying the check, he asked the question that was driving him crazy. "Ruby, what exactly is it that Casey . . . Strawberry . . . has under control?"

"Finding out where that thing about your paper got started," Ruby answered, her expression and tone suggesting she was surprised he had to ask. She glanced at her watch, then smiled encouragingly at Alex. "Your girl's probably at the Club See-More right about now, as a matter of fact. She told Smiley she'd be over there around two this afternoon."

Alex blanched and leapt to his feet. "Club See-More? And you let her go?"

"*Let* her go?" Ruby protested. "What am I, her den mother? I can make sure she cleans her plate, maybe, but where she goes is up to her."

"Sorry," Alex said hastily. "It's just that . . . Club See-More? You're sure? Why would Casey want to go there? Why would she even go near a strip joint?"

"Because that's where she tracked the rumor to," Ruby said with a palms-up shrug. "Hey, you're really worried about the kid, huh? That's sweet, handsome. Not many fellas nowadays—"

Impulsively Alex leaned over the counter and planted a quick kiss on Ruby's cheek. "Smiley was right about the soup," he said hurriedly as he straightened up and started toward the door. "You outdid yourself. Now, can I ask a big favor?"

"You got it, honey."

"If Casey shows up around here in the next couple of hours without me, would you tell her to check in with the answering machine at the paper and keep checking until we connect?"

"Sure. And maybe you could let me know if you do catch up with her," Ruby said. "Now you've got *me* worried. I had the feeling she could take care of herself, but you do hear stories about things that can happen to innocent . . ."

Alex didn't wait to hear the rest. He could fill in enough lurid details without any help from Ruby.

The strip club was a fifteen-minute fast-walk away, in the downtown core. Alex was tempted to go home for his car, but the Saturday-afternoon traffic was moving slowly. Since the rain had stopped, he decided he'd be better off on foot.

He wasn't sure what he intended to do when he reached the See-More. He didn't want to play the heavy with Casey again, but he would have to impress upon her that she just didn't understand certain things about Vancouver. If his warning made her angry, so be it. If she felt he was interfering with what she did on her own time, he'd remind her that *she* was interfering with *his* problem. And while he was at it, he told himself as he mentally rehearsed their probable quarrel, he would point out that he was still the damn boss!

He covered the distance to the club in ten minutes, slowing down only when he was approaching the brown-painted exterior of the large run-down building that housed the See-More along with a pawn shop on one side and an adult bookstore on the other.

Still uncertain how to handle the situation, Alex found himself hesitating outside the door of the strip club like an embarrassed would-be voyeur trying to work up the courage to go inside for the matinee. If Casey was in this place, he thought, where would he find her? In the audience? In a back room somewhere? Was she being leered at? Or worse? His hands clenched into fists as he paced furiously back and forth, arguing with himself. He was acting like an idiot again, one side of him insisted. If he let his imagination go any wilder, he'd be envisioning Casey tied hand and foot and tossed into the hold of a ship bound for a slave market somewhere, for pete's sake! What had possessed him to come chasing after her as if he had the right? But he *did* have the right, his other side protested. Not only the right, but the responsibility to take care of Casey, as her employer if not as her—

He put an abrupt stop to that line of thought. It was full of emotional land mines. He had to stay calm. Be logical.

And logic said that he had to go into that club and drag Casey out by the ear if necessary!

He started for the door.

"Is this how you spend your Saturday afternoons?" he heard.

Alex's heart slammed against the wall of his chest. *Casey.* But why was her voice coming from the sidewalk behind him? He turned, disoriented, then stood gaping at her. The dampness in the air had turned her red gold hair into an ethereal cloud of soft curls, and her eyes were the intense green of an exotic rain forest.

Gradually Alex noticed that Casey was dressed in low-heeled shoes and a prudish chambray shirt dress, with the bodice buttoned all the way up to a lace Peter Pan collar. She'd flung a red sweater over her shoulders and looped the sleeves loosely around her neck, and she clutched a plaid umbrella in her hand like a billy club. She looked as out of place as a Sunday-school teacher cruising Hollywood Boulevard, but Alex had a feeling her prim look was no accident. It was a clear case of defensive dressing. What she didn't seem to realize, he mused, as his body leapt in response to the very sight of her, was that trying to play down her sensual loveliness only emphasized it.

Overwhelmed by a flood of tenderness, Alex had to swallow a sudden lump in his throat before he could speak. "Where did you come from?" he finally asked.

"The pawn shop," Casey answered, battling an urge to fly into Alex's arms. In his white slacks and bright yellow jacket he looked clean and wholesome, strong, reassuring—her own personal ray of warm sunshine in the midst of this dreary neighborhood. "Where did *you* come from?"

"The diner. Ruby said I'd find you at the See-More. I . . . well, I was worried." Casey opened her mouth to speak, but Alex held out his hands as if to fend off her objections. "I know, Casey, I know. You can take care of yourself, you're a capable adult, you're an experienced reporter, you're . . ."

"Awfully glad to see you," Casey put in with a smile.

Alex stared at her again, taken aback. "You are?"

"This neighborhood's a bit . . . unnerving," she admitted. "I've discovered that it's one thing to know my way around the rough areas of cities I'm familiar with, but another matter altogether in places I've never been."

Alex hoped Casey couldn't see that he was still breathing hard from his Keystone Kops dash to save her from the fate worse than death he'd been picturing. He took her hand, tucked it under his arm, and started walking, firmly leading her away from the seedy street. "Vancouver's a great city, and for normal people it's a perfectly safe one, but you do seem to have a knack for gravitating to its few trouble spots, Strawberry." Hearing a telltale hoarseness in his voice, he cleared his throat and added, "I realize, of course, that you took on this mission on my behalf, and I'm still of two minds about whether to thank you or ground you at a desk job. Do you want to fill me in on the connection between some accountant's gossip mongering about *The Weekender*'s financial picture and a down-and-dirty strip club, a porno store, and a pawn shop? Where do these places fit in?"

"I'm not sure, exactly," Casey answered. "I mean, the obvious tie-in is that one of those two young men Smiley overheard talking about the paper happens to work in the See-More's office every Saturday afternoon." She shook her head and laughed quietly. "It turns out that our junior accountants are really MBA students who've set themselves up as part-time book-keepers for small businesses whose regular people are on vacation. They're good kids, really. They just need to learn a little discretion—and perhaps be a little choosier about their clients."

The muscles in Alex's arm suddenly flexed against Casey's hand, as if to draw her a little closer to his side.

She darted him a puzzled frown, then noticed two leather-clad, heavily booted skinheads rounding a corner just ahead and giving them a speculative once-over.

Casey wondered what might have happened if she'd been alone when she'd encountered this pair. They were clearly looking for trouble. Watching them she saw a grudging respect in their eyes as they checked Alex out. It struck her that she'd seen the same flicker of doubt in the expressions of the hard hats at the Dawson site, as if even their four-to-one odds hadn't been enough to dispel their worries about how much damage Alex might inflict before he was through.

In some ways Alex seemed to be such a gentle, urbane, civilized man, Casey reflected with a strange sense of pride. Yet under his smooth veneer was that unmistakable suggestion of a tough, unpredictable male it would be better not to mess with. She sensed it, Brittany had spotted it, and other males recognized it: The skinheads were giving him a wide berth.

Excitement sizzled its way along Casey's spine and sent a tingling warmth all the way down to her toes and out to her fingertips. It formed a tight nucleus of heat between her thighs and turned her blood to liquid fire. It was all she could do to keep walking, talking, pretending her world was normal.

"I'm a little confused, Casey," Alex said after he was certain there wasn't going to be any trouble.

He was confused? she thought, but merely raised a questioning brow and smiled at him.

"So what's the story here? How did you find out who those accountants were?"

Casey pulled herself together to explain the events of the previous afternoon at the diner, when she'd managed to get talking to Chris—the awkward youth who wasn't very good at crossword puzzles. Chris had, however, been very good at telling her everything he knew. He'd boasted about the bookkeeping business he and his buddy Eric had put together, and he'd crowed over having stuck Eric with the Saturday clerking stints at the infamous Club See-More.

"So you dropped in to see Eric at the club," Alex

said, trying to keep his attention focused on Casey's story despite the waves of emotion that were washing over him. "How did you get the kid to talk to you?" he asked absently.

"I told him I was from *The Weekender* and wanted to write a story on ambitious college students involved in offbeat summer projects—which I'd like to do, actually. If would be an interesting feature, don't you think?"

Alex nodded his agreement. "Did Eric say anything to you about how he'd gotten the idea our paper was about to fold?"

Our paper, Casey repeated silently, surprised that Alex would phrase it that way. It was just a figure of speech, of course, but still . . . "Eric warned me to find another job, as a matter of fact," she answered hastily when she realized she'd drifted off for a few seconds. With a mischievous grin she added, "The See-More's manager—his name's Frankie something—suggested that with a little loosening up of my image, the right costume, a couple of hours of bump-and-grind practice, I could probably handle a feature spot at the club."

"Billed as Strawberry Fields, no doubt?" Alex said lightly, trying not to let on how the very thought of Casey setting foot on that stage made him want to go back and punch out every patron in the place. And Frankie, the manager who'd had the gall to suggest such a thing to her, would rate special treatment. . . .

"Alex?" Casey said, her smile tentative. "I did refuse the gentleman's offer, you know."

Managing a laugh Alex told himself to settle down. This streak of possessiveness Casey aroused wasn't like him. Once again he dragged his attention back to the issue he and Casey were supposed to be discussing, and this time he doggedly stuck to the point. "So both Eric and this Frankie character told you to jump ship before your job disappeared out from under you?"

Casey nodded. "Frankie had put the bug in Eric's ear that *The Weekender*'s days were numbered. Frankie was gleeful about it. Apparently you've refused to accept ads from the club."

"I have," Alex said, then frowned and shook his head. "But for him to start a rumor that I'm on the brink of closing down? It seems like an excessively hostile reaction, doesn't it?"

"I don't think Frankie started the rumor," Casey said pensively. "He just passed it on. When I asked him where he'd heard it, all he would say was that it had come from an unpeachable source." She grinned. "That's what he said. Unpeachable. The pawn-shop owner was a lot more helpful. He told me he'd heard the same story from the man who collects his rent. A real-estate rep. I don't know whether you noticed, but the club, the adult bookstore, and the pawn shop are all part of the same building."

"What real-estate firm?" Alex asked, suddenly tense with expectation. "It wouldn't be a Dawson holding, would it?"

Casey shook her head. "Could be, but I'm not sure at this point. It's a numbered company."

Patting her hand Alex smiled. "You did well, Casey," he said, trying to hide his disappointment at the dead end she'd run into. "You dug up a lot of information, and you did it in hostile territory."

"Including," Casey said with a slow, satisfied grin, "the number of the company."

Stopping in his tracks Alex turned to search her eyes. "You're kidding."

"No, I'm not. When I went in to the See-More office

to visit Eric, he was doing ledger entries. The old-fashioned way, by hand. He was neatly recording all sorts of expense checks, including rents. His writing is legible even—"

"Upside down," Alex supplied with sudden excitement, curving his hands around Casey's upper arms. "Good lord, you were in a place like that, and you had the presence of mind to use that old journalist's trick? Casey McIntyre, you're fantastic! You're too good to be true! You're . . ." His words trailed off as he saw that Casey was looking past him, frowning. "What's the matter?" he asked, turning his head to follow her troubled gaze.

"There's a little boy running toward us crying his eyes out," she answered.

Alex saw who the youngster was and groaned inwardly.

Unless he missed his guess, another phase of the dirty-tricks campaign had been put into action.

Six

"Easy, Scotty," Alex said as the distraught boy stopped short of hurtling into him. "What's the matter? There's nothing wrong at home, is there?"

Shaking his head, Scotty swiped at one tear-stained cheek with the back of his hand and sniffed loudly.

Alex hunkered down to Scotty's level and ruffled the youngster's brown hair. "Then whatever the problem is, we can solve it, okay?"

"Okay," Scotty said, his bottom lip quivering. "It's my papers. Some guy grabbed my bundle and took off to the park. I chased after him, but he was bigger'n me, and I couldn't catch up. He dumped the whole pile in the bushes in the park and spread them around so every paper got all wet and ruined from the rain. Now I can't do my route."

"Sure you can," Alex countered. "We always print extras. You show me where your bundle ended up so you and I can clean up the mess, and then we'll come back here, get another stack of papers, and I'll help you deliver them."

Casey was astonished by Alex's offer. She knew by

now that the publisher of *The Weekender* was a breed apart from any other she'd ever run across. But to deliver papers? "*We'll* help," she said automatically.

Alex chuckled and shook his head as he straightened up, his gaze locked on Casey's. "*We'll* help," he repeated, his voice low and husky.

As they smiled at each other, Casey knew a bond was being forged between them, fragile but potentially strong, spun from the steel of honest friendship.

Finally Alex looked away and lightly touched the delivery boy's thin shoulder. "Okay, Scotty, lead us to the scene of the crime," he said with a wink that turned the youngster's small disaster into an adventure.

On the way to the park, Alex gently coaxed the details from Scotty, but didn't learn anything more specific than that a "real mean guy" had been the culprit.

"Alex, does this sort of thing happen often?" Casey asked when he'd given up on quizzing the boy. "You seem to be taking it in stride."

"You have to be prepared to deal with vandals and garden-variety mischief making in this business," he answered carefully. "It's part of the down side of running your own paper."

Casey realized that Alex didn't want to discuss the possible implications of this particular act of vandalism in front of Scotty, so she let the subject drop.

After stopping for plastic bags at a corner store near the park, they found the sodden papers, stuffed them into one of the giant bags, and deposited the whole thing in a nearby waste container.

When they got back to *The Weekender*, Alex slipped into his office to check messages and, as he rather sheepishly explained, to phone Ruby and report that Casey had survived her Club See-More visit.

With a bemused smile, Casey took Scotty down the hallway to the back of the house, where the former kitchen and pantry served as a delivery depot and warehouse for back issues.

Casey wasn't sure where the current papers were, and the "circulation manager"—an ambitious journalism student named Kirk Bishop, who worked Saturdays distributing the bundles of *The Weekender* to the delivery boys and retail outlets—had already finished his job, put everything away in its proper spot, and left.

She'd just found one of the day's stacks when Alex walked in. With one look at the familiar, tense muscle working in his jaw, Casey knew they had more than garden-variety mischief on their hands. "What's up?" she asked quietly.

"Kirk phoned. What happened to Scotty happened to three of our other kids. Young toughs grabbed the bundles and ditched them where they'd be ruined."

Casey blanched. "Four routes? Do you have enough extras to cover that much territory?"

"It's not quite as bad as it sounds," Alex answered, raking his fingers through his hair and glancing around as if to check how many extras they did have. "The individual routes aren't extensive. All the youngsters are around Scotty's age, so we use more of them and give them smaller areas to cover. But we'll definitely have to scrounge to get enough papers together. Luckily Kirk was about to start making the newsstand and corner store drops, so he still has all those bundles. He's coming right back here with them, and he's asked the kids in question to show up as well. We'll do a rob-Peter-to-pay-Paul redistribu-

tion so we can at least take care of our subscribers."
He managed a strained grin. "If you're still game and
have no other plans, we could use you now, Casey. It's
important for the kids to finish their routes themselves, but they'll need help so they won't be kept out
late."

"Still game? Just try to get rid of me," Casey
answered. "I'll call Brittany so there'll be an adult for
each child. She and I were talking about getting
together tonight for a movie or something anyway,
and she'll get a kick out of pitching in to help with
this sort of thing." Seeing that Alex was about to
protest, she lightly pressed two fingers to his lips,
smiled, and shook her head. "Don't bother arguing
with me, Alex. It's been said, with some justification,
that I'm a little bullheaded."

Her comment sounded vaguely familiar to Alex, but
he didn't remember where he'd heard it until Casey
winked at him, turned on her heel, and sauntered
out to the front office to make her call.

Casey was in her kitchen while Alex lounged comfortably on the floral couch in the living room, his
head resting on a soft cushion, his tired brain trying
to sort out how he'd ended up in this position despite
his best intentions.

It seemed to have happened so naturally, almost
without his noticing. Casey's place was the most
central to all the routes, and she'd suggested gathering there for pizza after the deliveries were made. The
kids were thrilled, their mothers readily gave permission, and a frantic scramble to counteract the latest
attack on the paper had turned into an impromptu
party. Brittany had suggested that Kirk could drive
her home as well as drop off the youngsters, and all of

a sudden the place had cleared out. "Take off your shoes and put your feet up, boss," Casey had said casually. "I'll go make us some tea."

To his utter astonishment he'd taken off his shoes and put his feet up.

Fortunately—or unfortunately—he was too bone tired to take advantage of being alone with Casey. Right now he wasn't sure which. He rubbed his eyes, trying to keep them open. He wanted to talk with Casey about everything that had happened. He wanted to share theories with her, hear all the details she hadn't told him yet, and simply enjoy being with her. Maybe if he quit fighting his exhaustion and closed his eyes for a couple of seconds, he could perk up enough to have some tea, summon one last burst of energy, and go home.

Right. Good idea. Just a couple of seconds . . .

Casey smiled and felt a disturbing tug at her heartstrings. Sound asleep, Alex looked so unguarded.

Quietly she put down the tea tray and slipped away to the bedroom to get a blanket. Perhaps she should wake him and send him home, she thought, but she didn't have the heart to disturb anyone who was so exhausted.

Moments later, as she was cautiously pulling a lightweight quilt over him, she had to battle a powerful temptation to brush a stray lock of his dark hair back from his forehead, drop soft kisses on his eyelids, and snuggle up beside him. But she supposed it wouldn't be right to take advantage of a hapless male when he was sleeping, so she tucked the coverlet around him, turned off the light, and carried her tea to bed, where she ultimately slept with unexpected ease, strangely comforted and warmed by the knowledge that Alex was nearby.

A car horn sounded outside, and Alex shot straight off the couch, totally disoriented as he stood looking around.

He winced with sudden understanding as he saw the rays of a bright late-morning sun streaming through the picture window on the opposite side of the room. Terrific, he thought disgustedly. He'd stayed all night with Casey—but not *with* Casey. He'd slept right through it all. Great. Nice going. She must have been thrilled with his sparkling company.

Trying not to make any noise, he folded the quilt and left it at the end of the couch, then smoothed down his hair as best he could, picked up his shoes, and tiptoed out of the living room toward the front door. The kitchen, to the right of the entryway, was empty. Alex figured Casey must be in the bedroom down the hall to the left. If she was sleeping, and he was very quiet, he might be able to make a clean getaway. There wasn't much hope she would forget she'd had an overnight guest, but if he didn't have to face her . . .

"Hi," she said softly, emerging from the bedroom.

Alex stopped dead, but his pulse thrummed like the wings of a startled falcon as Casey leaned against the entryway wall. Dressed in a red T-shirt and khaki shorts, her hair damp from the shower and her makeup minimal, she looked positively sexy, her inviting lips curved in a sweet smile.

Alex's gaze swept over her. He noticed her full breasts outlined through the cloth of her shirt, and her lightly tanned legs, which were coltishly graceful. She took his breath away. "I didn't make a sound," he protested, as if she'd somehow betrayed him by intercepting his escape and arousing his desire before he'd had a chance to get it under control.

"I know. But I was already up, and I was coming in to see if you'd regained consciousness yet," Casey said, suspecting that the effects of the heat that Alex's intense scrutiny had sent sizzling through her body were visible. "The main bathroom in this place is off my bedroom, far enough away so I could shower without waking you," she went on with deceptive calm. The erotic fantasies she'd indulged in while the warm water streamed over her naked body, with Alex just a room away, still had her in turmoil. "You really slept. You must have been awfully tired."

"I was, but that's no excuse . . ."

"Alex, please," Casey said, her eyes glinting with wicked humor. "No morning-after regrets, okay?"

"Regrets?" he echoed, frowning in sudden confusion.

Casey pushed off from the wall and moved toward him. "Don't worry, boss. Your virtue is still intact." She touched her index finger to the shallow cleft in his chin. "And yes, I still respect you in the morning."

Before Alex could react, Casey had moved past him and was heading for the kitchen. "While I rustle up some breakfast, you're welcome to use the shower. I've put out towels, a disposable razor, and a toothbrush for you. I read somewhere that a person should change toothbrushes every couple of weeks, so I stocked up on spares during a drugstore special I read about in *The Weekender*." She glanced back over her shoulder and grinned. "I believe in supporting the advertisers who help pay my salary."

"You would," Alex said, shaking his head and laughing. Disarmed by her teasing he felt the fight going out of him, his resistance gradually slipping away. Wanting Casey seemed to have become a permanent condition, and it was getting more and more difficult to remember why he should keep a lid on his feelings.

Giving up on the escape plan, he decided he'd like very much to use the shower off Casey's bedroom. The intimacy of it was oddly appealing to him. In deference to his common sense, however, he chose to make his shower a cold one.

It didn't do a bit of good. He still wanted her. Maybe more than ever.

"Ruby would have a fit if she knew about this breakfast," Casey said as she and Alex polished off the last of their sausage, eggs, and buttered toast. "But I fall off the low-cholesterol wagon only once in a while, so I don't feel too guilty."

Alex grinned. "I wonder if Smiley's doctor realizes that when he ordered his patient to watch his fat intake, he was going to change the eating habits of an entire neighborhood. As far as Ruby's concerned . . ."

"What's good for Smiley is good for everybody," Casey said at the same time Alex did.

As they laughed, it occurred to Alex that being with Casey—no matter what they were doing or what was going on—was always a kind of celebration. Her zest and humor were a tonic. She made him realize that somewhere along the way he'd started taking himself and everything else much too seriously.

Contentedly sipping his coffee, he decided he wanted to know more about her. Much, much more. But where to start? How? "It's great the way you've settled into the West End community," he commented as a way to focus the conversation on her. "You really seem to be part of things here. I have trouble remembering you've been in town just over a month."

"I've been lucky," Casey said with a little shrug. "Brittany paved the way for me. When she came to Vancouver a few months ago, she was on her own. By the time I arrived, she'd sorted out the elements that turn a neighborhood into a home. Take The Starting Gate. Smiley and Ruby were fond of Britt, so right away they made me feel I belonged too."

"That's important to you," Alex said, probing a little. "Belonging, I mean. Feeling at home."

Casey suddenly felt self-conscious. "I suppose so," she admitted.

"Yet you've told me that independence is the most important thing of all to you," Alex pointed out. "Is it possible to have both?"

Casey shifted uncomfortably in her chair. Alex had zeroed right in on the dichotomy that kept her in a chronic state of discontent. "I was raised to be independent," she said, though she knew she wasn't answering the question.

"And did you also grow up with that feeling of belonging you treasure so much?" Alex asked gently, sensing that he'd stumbled onto something important.

Casey opened her mouth to gloss over her answer, but something made her choose to be more honest with Alex. More open. "Not really," she admitted. "Ours wasn't a very happy household. I felt more at home with Brittany's folks and several understanding neighbors. My parents have never gotten along. Their marriage seems to have been a mistake from the beginning, and I was, to be blunt about it, an accident compounding that mistake. They stayed together because of an old-fashioned belief that a child deserved something better than a broken home. As a teenager I tried to convince them that our home *was* broken, and a separation or divorce would be like repair work, but they stuck it out, poor things, and now they don't seem to want to live without each other. I guess the anger is better than the unknown."

Alex found himself caught in a maelstrom of raw emotion. Except for the small clue of Casey's fierce need for independence, he'd have given odds that someone so open and upbeat must have had a storybook childhood. She obviously hadn't, yet there was no cynicism in her. Only compassion and a loving nature. He thought about his own happy-go-lucky upbringing in the lively McLean household. His disappointments had come later, mainly of his own making, yet hadn't he allowed them to erode his natural optimism?

He could learn a great deal, he realized, from this woman.

Casey saw a darkening of Alex's eyes and a warmth in his expression that set off a small panic inside her, and she suddenly jumped up to bustle around in the kitchen. "I wonder if Ron will be back to work tomorrow," she said brightly, changing the subject with as much subtlety as a rampaging bulldozer altering a landscape.

Alex watched her for several moments in silence, still stunned by the intensity of the feelings that gripped him. He longed to go to Casey and draw her into his arms, for once not in passion but in . . . *Stop right there,* he ordered himself. "Perhaps I should check the messages back at the office," he said aloud, getting to his feet. "May I use your phone?"

"Go right ahead," Casey answered with a polite smile.

Alex went to the living room and made the call, barely aware of his automatic motions. He wasn't very proud of the way he'd just withdrawn from Casey, when what he'd wanted was to get closer to her—and when she'd offered him that chance, in her shy and tentative way. The Alex McLean he'd once been wouldn't have chosen a superficial display of manners in place of honest feeling.

But he wasn't that Alex McLean anymore. He was a man with little to recommend him but a business that demanded all his time and energy, a financial future that could easily end up awash in red ink, and a cantankerous streak no woman would put up with for long.

The message on the office answering-machine tape put a sudden stop to his musings. He listened, hung up, sat staring into space for several moments, finally gave his head a shake, and went back to the kitchen.

"Uh-oh," Casey said as soon as she looked up from washing the dishes. "What now?"

Alex picked up a tea towel and a plate and started drying. "Ron's wife phoned," he said after a long moment. "You were right to tell him to go to the hospital when he took sick. Unfortunately, he didn't take your advice until yesterday, and then he went to emergency only because he was in such pain he had no choice. It turns out he didn't have the flu after all."

Casey caught her breath. "What's wrong with him?"

"Appendix. The damn fool was so determined not to give in to being ill, he made it to the operating table just in time. He barely missed out on a rupture."

"Good lord, is he all right?"

"He's fine. But . . ." Alex smiled ruefully. "He'll be out of action for at least a couple of weeks."

Casey's heart began pounding so hard, it was reverberating in her ears. She hadn't expected such a challenge so early in her new career. And she'd been counting on Ron to be a buffer between herself and Alex. Now, all of a sudden, she was on her own.

But first things first, she told herself firmly. Instead of thinking about herself, she might consider reassuring Alex. He had to be wondering what would be thrown at him next. "I can handle things, boss," she said with all the bravado she could muster. "No problem. A piece of cake."

Alex put down the dish towel, curved one hand around her shoulder, and smoothed his palm over her cheek, his fingers gently combing back several wayward curls that had tumbled forward. Searching the fern green depths of her eyes, thinking about how he would have no choice but to depend on Casey and probably work very closely with her for the next little while, he found himself wondering if fate was trying to tell him something. "I know you can keep things going," he said, touched by this latest evidence of her unswerving loyalty. "But remember, I'm part of this team too. So *we'll* handle this one, Strawberry—just as we've handled everything else. *We* will. Understand?"

Casey nodded almost imperceptibly, transfixed by the heat of Alex's gaze, the possessiveness of his touch.

She waited breathlessly, every nerve in her body taut with anticipation, her lips parting in eager readiness . . .

But Alex lowered his hands and, to Casey's frustration, went back to drying dishes.

She was gripped by a sudden urge to break every plate over his thick head.

Their work week began with a quick hospital visit. Marie Coulter had asked Alex and Casey to drop in to see her husband. Even though Ron was still dazed from his surgery, he wouldn't settle down until he was certain everything at the paper was under control.

Casey traded her shorts and top for taupe linen slacks and a lacy crocheted sweater, then walked with Alex to *The Weekender* building so he could change his clothes and pick up his car. On the way they had a mild argument about the divvying up of chores. Alex wanted to shoulder most of the burden in addition to everything else he had to do. Casey insisted that he could stick to whatever schedule he'd followed when Ron was on the job.

At the hospital Ron got in on the act as well, dictating a list of instructions and reminders to both Alex and Casey while Alex took notes as if he were the employee and Ron the boss.

The discussion of who should do what became a recurring theme for the next several days. Alex was amazed by how little assistance Casey wanted from him, while she was surprised and secretly pleased by how much help he gave her. For both of them a welcome by-product of their hectic days was that their unsettling personal feelings took a backseat to the demands of the job.

For Casey there were neighborhood events to be reported on and photographed. She had to edit copy from free-lancers, look at a barrage of press releases and reader letters that arrived at the office, and prepare the usable ones for typesetting, all the while handling countless other niggling chores she'd never given a thought to before. A weekly newspaper editor's work, she soon discovered, was never done.

For Alex there were conferences with his accountant, the usual visits to his smallest and newest papers in the suburbs, lunches with advertisers, and strategy sessions with his salesmen—whose reports confirmed his suspicions about the stolen newspaper bundles.

"Imagine," Marg Abbott said indignantly on Thursday afternoon as she placed several columns of type on Casey's composing-room worktable. "Just *imagine* anyone being so rotten!"

Looking up from a press release she was editing, Casey blinked several times, focusing her thoughts as well as her eyes. "Rotten? Who's rotten?"

"Didn't Alex tell you?" Sandra piped up without missing a beat, her fingers flying over her keyboard just as Marg's were on hers—the Ferrante and Teicher of typesetting, Casey fondly called the two women.

"The salesmen from *The English Bay Gazette* have been going around all week to our advertisers with Polaroids of *The Weekender* lying in ditches," Marg explained. "They're saying our circulation isn't what we claim it is. They're also saying they managed to get the pictures because they just happened to see our kids dumping instead of delivering."

Sandra gave a highly unladylike snort. "In a pig's eye it just happened," she blurted, then turned beet red over her uncharacteristic outburst.

Casey and Marg exchanged a glance, then laughed delightedly. Sandra was normally such a quiet little mouse, Casey thought, pleased by the woman's unexpected feistiness. It was another example of the loyalty Alex commanded.

As Marg and Sandra went on with a gloating review of how masterfully Alex had handled the situation, Casey only half listened, pensively worrying at her lower lip. Alex had told her about what the salesmen from *The Gazette* were doing, but he'd predicted it long before he'd heard the feedback. As far back as Sunday afternoon, after they'd left the hospital, he'd told her exactly what to expect. He'd even suggested that the publisher of *The Gazette* had arranged for young hoodlums to snatch the papers. It was a tough accusation to prove, and probably not worth the time or effort it would take. But Alex had armed his salesmen with evidence that *The Weekender* had indeed been delivered to its subscribers, so the whole nasty trick had backfired.

Casey's admiration for Alex was beginning to know no bounds. "It's hard to believe any businessman has to stoop so low to beat out a competitor," she murmured after the chatter between the other two women died down. A theory was taking shape in her mind. It seemed farfetched, yet it would explain the implausible coincidence of there being so many attacks on Alex from so many different directions. She just wished she had time to check it out.

"What really burns me," Marg said with an edge that commanded Casey's attention, "is that anybody would pick on such little kids that way. When I think of poor Scotty crying his eyes out last Saturday, I want to throttle the person responsible."

Casey tapped the eraser end of her pencil against her chin. Marg had brought up something that made her curious, so she asked about it: "Why *are* all our kids so young, by the way? They seem to do a great job, but I've never seen a paper where all the delivery boys and girls seem to be under twelve. Is there a reason, or did it just work out that way by chance?"

"There's a reason," Marg answered. "They're all from what I guess you'd call disadvantaged homes. Alex is part of an informal business group that tries to help people in trouble help themselves, in a way that rebuilds their pride. Since most of the bigger kids can get jobs at fast-food restaurants or in stores or even delivering for the larger newspapers, Alex makes a point of hiring the younger brothers and sisters and tailoring the routes to what they can handle."

Casey abruptly returned her attention to her press release. She really hadn't needed to hear any more about how wonderful Alex was. She already knew enough. If she listened to another word, she might slip right over the edge of the abyss she dreaded above all: She might fall in love with him. And then where would she be?

Truly in love for the first time in her life, that was where.

With a man who did everything but perform back handsprings away from her every time they inched too close to each other.

Seven

"Casey, what do you think you're doing?"

She looked up, caught off guard. Alex stood inside the composing-room door, a slight five-o'clock shadow dusting the stubborn set of his jawline. But it wasn't five o'clock, Casey thought guiltily. It was six-thirty, and everyone else had left the office ages ago.

She smoothed down the ad she'd placed on a cardboard flat and forced herself to seem unruffled despite swearing under her breath. Alex had been out at meetings all afternoon, and she'd expected him to have dinner with a client. He'd left the office wearing a suit and tie, a signal every other day so far this week that he was on his way to do some heavy-duty advertiser courting. Alex, she'd noticed, was more than devoted to his company. He was a man obsessed.

But he'd fooled her this evening. He'd come back to *The Weekender* in time to catch her breaking his cardinal rule. Now she was in for it.

She decided her best approach was to treat the situation lightly. "What do I think I'm doing?" she repeated in a deadpan monotone. "I think I'm getting a jump on this week's pasteup. I think I'm trying to make sure I meet the deadline. I think I'm hearing the beginnings of another don't-ever-work-alone-in-the-office speech from the boss, and probably an order to haul my butt out of here right now or else."

"Good thinking," Alex shot back, covering the distance between them in three long strides. He was planning to seize both Casey's hands in his, pull her to her feet, and deliver a lecture she wouldn't ignore next time. But when he saw that she had her toes hooked behind the bottom rung of her perch, he shifted gears and went for a more straightforward tactic. Bending down he slid one arm behind Casey's back and the other under her legs to disentangle them from the stool, then straightened up and carried her toward the door.

A trill of startled laughter bubbled up from deep inside Casey as she threw one arm around Alex's neck and hung on for dear life. "You can't carry me, you ninny," she said with a giggle. "I'm too heavy."

Alex stopped short. He gaped at her, his eyes dark with shock as he realized what he'd done. The frayed thread of self-discipline that had kept him in line for nearly a week had snapped. "You're not heavy," he said in a barely audible rasp. "Not at all. But . . . what the devil am I doing *now*? Dammit, Casey, I can't be alone with you for thirty seconds without losing every ounce of sense I've ever had!"

Casey's eyes flashed with sudden anger. Alex was on the verge of putting her down! After jump-starting her pulse and instantaneously revving up her sensual motor, he was going to set her back on her feet, give her the equivalent of a pat on the head, and send her on her way!

Not this time, she decided abruptly. "Damn you,

Alex McLean," she said, cupping her free hand behind his head and drawing it downward until she captured his tempting mouth with hers.

His lips were stiff at first, as if he intended to fight off the sudden onslaught. But when his arms tightened around her and a helpless groan tore from his throat, she felt a burst of female power. She swept her tongue back and forth over his lower lip, then the upper one, stroking the rigidity away. She teased at their moist inner flesh until she'd coaxed them apart. Tasting the familiar hot sweetness of his mouth, Casey realized how desperately she'd been craving it . . . craving *him*. She invaded, explored, feasted, and savored with mindless, dizzy joy.

Gradually Alex's resistance was transformed to enthusiastic participation. In the midst of taking, Casey found herself giving. It was Alex who was beginning to make demands, Alex's mouth possessing hers, Alex's tongue tormenting and thrusting.

Then, still holding her in his arms, he was striding purposefully out of the room into the hallway. Dazed with surprise and pleasure, Casey nuzzled into a warm hollow of his throat, pressing kisses to a throbbing pulse spot and lapping like a hungry kitten at his spice-scented skin. Her fingers fumbled to loosen his tie and work open enough of his shirt buttons to let her hand slide under the crisp cotton. The coarse silk of his chest hair was pleasantly scratchy against her fingertips, and his hard nipples leapt to her touch.

She heard the sharp intake of Alex's breath, but she knew the sound had nothing to do with the exertion of carrying her. He ascended the stairs to his apartment quickly and easily, as if she were weightless in his arms. Flattening her palm over the mat of hair covering his breastbone, she felt the strong, steady rhythm of his heartbeat. The deep reservoir of strength he could draw on amazed Casey—and thrilled her in some secret, primitive recess of her femininity.

He hadn't locked his apartment, so he had no trouble opening the door, then kicking it shut behind them.

Casey didn't notice the furniture this time. Her surroundings consisted of Alex, and only Alex. When she felt herself being lowered onto a mattress, she had no curiosity about the bed or the room. Nothing mattered but that Alex was covering her mouth with his while his hands were deftly, quickly undressing her.

Turnabout was fair play, she thought as she frantically helped him on his way to glorious nakedness. Clothes flew in all directions, landing on the floor on both sides of the bed, on the dresser across the room, on a night-table lamp. Kisses were fierce, caresses impatient and possessive, whispered words demanding, pleading, urging.

Alex wanted to slow down. He'd been tearing around like a cornered fox all week, using trumped-up client dinners and meetings and any other excuse he could think of to stay out of temptation's way and give him time to think rationally about Casey. Now that he'd succumbed, now that he'd accepted the inevitable, it seemed like a waste to race, and totally unnecessary. He wasn't going to back off at this point, and Casey wasn't showing signs of changing her mind.

But desire was pounding through him like a torrent cascading over a crumbling dam, and Casey was arching under him, making him throb almost painfully with the need to plunge into her and feel her moist flesh closing around him.

AFTER HOURS • 103

He fought to keep control. He wanted to pleasure Casey, wanted to appreciate her to the fullest and make her lose herself to an all-consuming ecstasy. "Patience, baby," he urged. But she'd started touching him in ways that were guaranteed to obliterate what little discipline he had left. "Patience," he said again, almost choking out the word. Typically she kept right on doing . . . what she was doing . . . so well.

Suddenly grabbing her hands and pinning them to the mattress on either side of her head, Alex rubbed his cheek over hers, then over the smooth swell of her breasts, murmuring in husky, soothing tones, "We have lots of time, sweetheart. I'm not going anywhere and neither are you. Let me love you properly."

Casey tried to calm herself, but the scratchiness of Alex's whiskers heightened her arousal. "I've *been* patient!" she blurted out, tearing her hands free and plunging her fingers into his dark hair. Twisting to present the engorged tip of one of her breasts to his mouth, she shuddered as she heard Alex's low chuckle and felt his lips closing over the sensitive nipple, his tongue swirling hotly around and over it. "Oh Alex, it's so good," she cried raggedly, her body undulating like the swell of an ocean wave. "So beautiful. But I need you! Oh please, I need you *now*!

Alex raised his head and gazed down at her in a moment of wonder. Something was surging through him. Something beyond desire but fueled by it. Something he hadn't felt for years, hadn't really known was missing until now, when it was flooding back. He was infused with a soaring confidence that was as essential to him as lifeblood. He realized that it was Casey who was restoring his vital sense of power. Casey, offering him her surrender as unstintingly as she'd given him her loyalty. All at once he was in full control. Whatever it took, Casey was going to experience every delight he could give her—whether or not the unleashed tigress she'd turned into was willing to settle down in purring contentment.

Recapturing her hands he cuffed her wrists with his fingers and pulled her arms up over her head, a position reminiscent of the way he'd imprisoned her that first night.

Her eyes were huge as she looked up at him, not in alarm but in puzzled, excited consternation.

"Casey, I told you to have patience," he said softly as he leaned down to savor the nipple he'd neglected so far, his free hand gliding possessively over her long, slender torso to the gentle flare of her hips, then slowly meandering toward the apex of her thighs. "And this is one time," he added when she bucked against his exploring fingers in a desperate demand, "when you'll do as I say and follow my lead—and like it."

Alex's implacable tone electrified Casey. She searched his eyes and saw a quiet resolve that stilled any protests she might have offered. "Whatever you say, boss," she said at last with a shaky laugh.

His hands were like a master sculptor's as they molded and shaped her contours. His lips mesmerized her as they brushed her eyelids, learned her features, and traveled downward over her body with feathery, tantalizing kisses. His tongue seared her like a brand, unerringly discovering secret places of excruciating sensitivity. He was merciless. He refused to let her cheat herself of sensual delights. He forced her to confront her own eroticism and revel in it.

Only when she was utterly and helplessly compliant did he release her wrists so she could begin touching him, stroking his back and shoulders, skimming her fingers over his muscular arms, and caressing the nape of his neck.

Casey was trembling from head to toe by the time Alex finally moved over her, sliding his arms under her body and cradling her with heart-stopping tenderness.

She twined her arms around his neck, her long legs around his hips. "Now?" she murmured, the single word charged with submissiveness and fiery need.

Alex hesitated long enough to imprint the perfect, precious moment on his memory. Then, cupping his hands under Casey's bottom to lift her hips, he nodded. "Now."

A half moan, half sigh escaped Casey when Alex's first deep thrust filled her. He paused to give her body a chance to adjust to his invasion, but she tightened her thighs and coaxed him deeper. Raining kisses over his face and throat and chest, her fingers sifting through his silky hair, Casey simply gave herself over to Alex, holding nothing back.

His tempo increased little by little. Casey caught his rhythm and went willingly wherever he led her. "Alex," she cried out when he'd carried her to a summit higher than she'd ever imagined she could climb. "Oh lord, Alex . . ."

"I'm here, sweetheart," he whispered. "I'm with you, baby. I won't let you go. I'm here." He kept murmuring endearments and holding her close, making her feel treasured and safe.

All at once there was a quickening of their joined bodies, a rush of intense heat inside her, a gathering of forces for an imminent explosion. Alex closed his mouth over hers and completed the circle of their fusion, and in that timeless, blindingly sublime moment, they were a single entity.

• • •

Casey nestled happily against Alex's broad, hard chest, her legs tangled with his, her body humming with contentment.

They were lying between the navy blue sheets, Alex half sitting and half lying on pillows propped against the polished oak headboard.

"You were right," she said as they luxuriated in the languorous aftermath of their profoundly satisfying lovemaking. "Following your lead has definite possibilities." Tilting her head back she smiled up at him. "I did like it."

Alex grinned, feeling pleased with himself and Casey and life in general. He toyed with a curl of her tousled hair, then brushed the backs of his fingers over her flushed cheek. "Consider it a lesson learned," he said teasingly. "You're impatient and impulsive and impetuous. You need a steadying hand."

"Well, yours is very nice," she said as she touched her lips to his palm. "Hardly steadying, however, considering the things this particular hand has made me do."

"How about this one?" Alex said, touching her with his other hand in a way that aroused her impatience, impulsiveness, and impetuousness all over again.

Casey gave a helpless little gasp, but managed to say playfully, "Your right hand's even worse. In fact . . ." She caught her breath again and closed her eyes. "In fact, it's positively depraved."

Maneuvering her with a quick, decisive move that ended with Casey straddling his thighs and looking down at him with a shocked expression, Alex gave her a wicked smile. "And do you have a problem with all that depravity?" he asked blandly.

Casey swallowed hard and shook her head, hardly daring to believe he was ready to make love to her again. "Not . . . not at the moment, it seems."

"Good." Alex reached up and let Casey's full breasts spill into his palms, gently kneading them.

Casey's spine arched instinctively, and she threw back her head as incredible sensations once again overcame her.

"You don't have to wait for permission," Alex said, his voice vibrating with male satisfaction as he saw how she responded to him. "You've had your lesson in patience. Now take what you want, Casey. Whatever you want, however you want it. This time—for a little while—you're the boss."

She knew what she wanted, and how she wanted it. She raised her hips, slowly lowered herself over Alex, and took him in until he was totally hers, then began moving, establishing her own rhythm.

And as she rode him, taking her pleasure as if he existed solely for her delight, Alex's wonderfully depraved hands performed their special magic.

Casey lounged lazily against the pillows, sated and blissfully content. She'd never experienced such a sense of well-being. She'd never known such exhilaration.

She sighed deeply as she heard Alex returning from taking the remains of their picnic in bed back to the kitchen. He was full of surprises, she mused. Given his habit of eating at diners and restaurants, she hadn't expected him to have anything remotely edible in his refrigerator, yet when they'd stopped making love for long enough to realize they were famished, he'd slipped away for a few minutes and returned with fruit, cheese, cold chicken, crusty bread, and chilled white wine. "I take care of myself very well," he'd explained with a grin, pretending he'd just happened to have such goodies on hand. When Casey hadn't believed a word of it, he'd confessed to having stocked up that morning after toying with the idea of inviting Casey to join him for another lunch in the park. She, however, had taken off for a noon press conference.

He appeared in the bedroom doorway and paused to look at her in a way that made her feel beautiful and desirable and special. She gave him a slow, languid smile. Comfortable with his nakedness, he seemed unaware of his own magnificence, but Casey fully appreciated his masculinity. The easy tailoring of his clothes had been deceptive, disguising his surprising muscularity. She'd known he was lean and taut, but she'd had no idea of his sheer physical power. No wonder he wasn't a man to back down from a street fight. And no wonder he'd had no trouble carrying her up the stairs to his bed.

Caught unaware by a rush of emotion she wasn't ready to deal with, Casey chose to take refuge in combativeness. "You know, boss, speaking of impatient, impetuous, impulsive people, you were the one who started all this debauchery, picking me up the way you did," she said with a wicked grin as he stretched out on the bed beside her. "Who do you think you are, Rhett Butler?"

Alex laughed and gathered her into his arms, loving the feel of Casey's soft body against him too much to let her escape for very long. "Thanks for reminding me," he said as sternly as he could. "We have to talk, Casey McIntyre. Or rather, I have to talk. You have to listen for once. The reason I picked you up in the first place was that you had no business being in that composing room by yourself. You were flouting my direct orders."

"I had to," she defended herself. "And I ought to march right back downstairs to finish what I started."

"What will it take to make you toe the line?" Alex asked with renewed frustration. "How can I get through to you that if somebody decides to break into our offices and finds you in the way, you could get hurt? Besides, why do you feel you need to get a jump on the pasteup? You found out last week that it only takes a morning to do the job."

"Sure, when you're on the scene," Casey agreed, snuggling cozily against Alex even as she argued with him. "But have you forgotten the publishers' conference in Seattle this weekend? Earlier today I overheard one of the salesmen saying the three of you were booked on a flight first thing tomorrow morning, so I wasn't about to bank on your help for this particular pasteup."

Alex placed three fingers under Casey's chin and tipped her head back so she was looking up at him. "Do you honestly think I'd leave you to handle the pasteup on your own? That I wouldn't even ask you if you felt you could manage? That I'd take a chance you'd work after hours to get it done?"

"Well, I guess I . . . I suppose I didn't think at all," Casey said, preferring not to admit she'd been a little hurt by Alex's apparent callousness, though she'd been trying to tell herself he simply had faith in her ability to do the job. She rested her head on his shoulder again. "But surely you're not going to miss the conference, are you?"

"I can't. It's too important, for any number of reasons. But I don't need to be there for the opening speeches and the rubber-chicken lunch, so I changed my flight. I don't leave until one." Alex frowned as the disturbing realization hit him that he'd taken for granted that Casey would know he'd never leave her in the lurch. But why should she know? And how much time would it have taken him to reassure her?

He didn't mean to be so oblivious. It just seemed to happen, a basic flaw in his character he'd never managed to overcome. It had contributed to the failure of his marriage, and already it was showing up in his relationship with Casey. "I'm sorry," he said, genuinely regretful. "I'd like to use the excuse that things have been so hectic, I haven't had a chance to fill you in on the arrangements I've made to back you up over the weekend, but there really isn't any excuse. I have a tendency to steamroll along without pausing for discussions. And we have a lot to discuss." Even as he spoke, he knew there was one arrangement he wouldn't tell Casey about. She would be livid. And he didn't care that his decision was another manifestation of the very tendency he was apologizing for. He was going ahead as planned.

Casey didn't answer at first. She was deeply disturbed by her reaction to Alex's news that he would be around for a half day longer than she'd expected. It wasn't merely that she was glad to be able to count on his help. She was going to miss him when he left. He would be away for just a weekend, and she was going to miss him.

It was the first sobering thought to intrude on the euphoria of the past few hours. Casey didn't like missing people. Especially male people. It meant she was becoming dependent, and she simply didn't permit herself that luxury. The whole thrust of her existence, for as long as she could remember, was to achieve as much autonomy as possible, in every way possible.

Suddenly, as if the effects of a powerful aphrodisiac had worn off, she saw the enormity of what she'd done. For ultracautious Casey McIntyre to have made love with a man after knowing him only a week was bad enough, but for her to have let down all her defenses and shed all her inhibitions the way she had with Alex was unthinkable. What was worse, he'd been reluctant from the start to let this craziness happen. What had possessed her to seduce him? Seduce? She'd practically *forced* herself on him!

Shifting out of Alex's arms, Casey propped herself up on one elbow and studied him, struggling to ignore the germ of an old, painfully familiar panic implanted deep inside her. She was astonished that her fears hadn't surfaced sooner. "I guess I sort of . . . well, had my way with you," she said carefully. "I mean, I know you didn't want this to happen between us, Alex."

"I *wanted* it to happen," he corrected her, running one finger along her arm from shoulder to wrist. "But I didn't *intend* it to."

Casey waited for him to expand on his comment, to give her some reason—any reason—why he hadn't *intended* to get involved with her this way. When he didn't offer one, she tried prompting him a little. "I hope I haven't caused any . . . complications . . . for you," she said in a small voice.

"Complications?" he repeated, leaning back with his hands clasped behind his head and closing his eyes. Casey had knocked the struts out from under him, turned his more-or-less comfortable existence upside down, and made him question every one of his priorities, and she was wondering if she'd caused complications? "Baby, you have no idea," he said with a quiet laugh.

Casey pushed herself all the way up to a sitting

position and pulled the sheet around her, clutching it over her breasts. "What else do we need to discuss about the weekend?" she asked abruptly.

"Casey?" Alex said, opening his eyes and giving her a puzzled look. "Casey, what's—"

"Are you concerned that there'll be problems with the deliveries again?" she interrupted. She didn't want to know what Alex meant. Whatever he meant, it all came down to the same thing: She'd created difficulties of some kind for him.

The germ of panic sprouted and started spreading through her like a nasty little weed.

Looking around at her scattered clothes, she wondered how she could retrieve them and keep her dignity at the same time. "Do you really believe *The Gazette* publisher would try vandalism a second time, after the first effort backfired so badly?" she asked automatically, her professional demeanor instantly back in place despite her personal distraction. Or maybe because of it. Work had always been her refuge.

"I doubt it, but whether or not he does, there'll be no problems with this weekend's deliveries," Alex said tersely. "I've seen to it." Realizing that Casey's sudden coolness was rooted in some inner conflict that had little or nothing to do with his failure to tell her about his changed flight plans, he tried teasing her, saying in an exaggerated growl, "Now get back here, Strawberry."

"No," Casey said with a forced smile. "Sorry, boss. I don't take orders in bed."

"How soon we forget," Alex murmured.

Casey reddened. She wished now she *could* forget how eagerly she'd obeyed Alex's every whispered command only a little while before. "Just tell me how you've seen to the delivery matter," she said in clipped syllables. "I think it's only right that your acting managing editor should be clued in on something that important." Out of the corner of her eye she spied her flowered silk shirt puddled on the floor right beside the bed. Perfect, she thought. The blouse was long enough to cover her hips. If she could get it and put it on, the challenge of gathering up the rest of her clothes would be easier to deal with.

Pulling the sheet more closely around her she poked her leg out to the side, stretched it down toward the floor, and slid her toe under the pool of silk.

Alex watched the whole covert action in mild fascination as he explained that he'd made special arrangements for keeping close tabs on the routes. He didn't supply details—and once again he omitted the particular detail that would send Casey straight through the ceiling. It wasn't something she needed to know.

He saw her graceful, silk-draped foot disappearing under the sheet, then her left hand tunneling to meet it.

"What arrangements?" she asked, slowly drawing her blouse toward her and keeping her gaze averted. She didn't want to face Alex.

Alex frowned. Did she think he wouldn't allow her to get dressed if she wanted to? Did she figure that if she didn't look at him, he couldn't see what she was doing? She was too pretty to be an ostrich, but she was acting like one. He continued watching her, his eyes narrowed. Fine, he told himself. If Casey chose to have hurt feelings and pretend *not* to have hurt feelings, far be it from him to force the issue.

"Why aren't you answering me?" Casey snapped. "Precisely what arrangements have you made about the deliveries?" She slipped her blouse out from under the sheet, determined to be wearing it within three seconds. "Damn, damn, *damn!*" she muttered. One of the long sleeves was inside out. And unless she let the sheet drop, she had only one hand available to rectify the situation.

Before she could figure out what to do, the blouse was whipped from her grasp and tossed aside, the sheet pulled away to expose her nakedness, and she was being tumbled onto her back with Alex stretching out full-length over her, pinning her hands over her head. His favorite position, she thought indignantly as she glared up at him, anger flaring in her green eyes. She only wished her body would start paying attention to what was going on in her mind. She was mad as blazes, but it was all she could do to restrain herself from twining her legs around Alex's hips and drawing him into her again!

"And now," Alex said firmly, surprising himself with his sudden decision that this particular woman wasn't going to leave him wondering what kind of male clumsiness he was guilty of, "we're going to have a little talk."

Eight

"What do you think I mean by complications?" Alex demanded, smiling down at Casey.

"I wasn't asking about complications," she said, wishing she'd kept her mouth shut about that subject. "I was talking about arrangements. The arrangements you say you've made about the deliveries."

"The hell you were. Be straight with me, Casey. What's bugging you?"

"Nothing. Never mind. It doesn't matter."

"It matters. Answer me."

"Quit giving me orders, Alex McLean!"

"I haven't even begun giving you orders the way I ought to, sweetheart. You've gotten away with being a rebel because you're gorgeous and funny and bright and well intentioned, but the fact is, you're a defiant imp, and it's long past time you *learned* to follow orders. So here's one for starters, my intrepid editor: I want your office key. I want it turned in to me before I leave for Seattle tomorrow. And *that's* an order."

Blanching, Casey stared up at Alex in horrified dismay. "Are you firing me? Has going to bed with me created such problems you want to turf me out even though you desperately need someone in Ron's place?"

Alex was taken aback by Casey's gross misinterpretation of his motives, but he was glad his shock tactic had thrown her off balance. Maybe now they could move past her stonewalling and get somewhere. "Of course I'm not firing you," he answered gently. "Do you think I'm a fool? I want your key, that's all. It seems to be the only way I can make sure you'll stay away from this place after hours."

"Oh," Casey said in a tiny voice, feeling foolish about the conclusion she'd jumped to.

Releasing her hands and resting most of his weight on one elbow, Alex began stroking her hair and brushing light kisses over her face as he spoke. "Let me tell you about this matter of complications, Casey, since it seems to bother you so much. What I'm talking about is that you've got me so worried about you, it's all I can do to keep my mind on anything else." He touched his lips to her temple and let his hand trail downward to caress her throat. The soft mist stealing over the brilliant emerald of her eyes told him that, whatever mysterious bee Casey had in her bonnet, she still wanted him as much as he wanted her. "As if there isn't enough going on around here to make me climb the walls," he continued, feeling he was on a roll with his affectionate scolding, "now I'm trying to keep tabs on a sweet, loyal, fearless blond who has a nose for trouble."

"You don't have to keep tabs on me," Casey said, though her protest lacked conviction. Alex's touch had a way of obliterating her self-will and soothing the fears he obviously didn't realize plagued her.

Believing he was making progress of some sort, Alex smiled. "I don't suppose it occurs to you that every minute you're out of my sight, I'm wondering if Vic Lundstrom and company have tracked you down with the intent of teaching both of us a lesson."

"That's silly." Casey laughed shakily, her hands fluttering to his shoulders. "You're still overreacting. By now those men have forgotten I exist."

"Sweetheart, you're not that forgettable." Alex pressed a kiss to the corner of her mouth and let his fingers stray to her breast, lightly stroking its silky underside. "And the Lundstrom contingent isn't the only problem. It scares the living daylights out of me to think that somebody from Club See-More or the numbered real-estate company that owns it might want to know why you were nosing around over there. Or that—"

"You're concerned about my safety?" Casey broke in, clasping her hands behind his neck. "That's the complication I've caused? That's it?"

"No, that's not it," Alex answered with exaggerated patience, rubbing his nose against hers. "Under the circumstances, concern for your safety would be the normal reaction of a responsible employer. What I'm talking about is being a crazy man. I want to tuck you into my pocket and take you wherever I go . . . or maybe handcuff our wrists together, or . . . or lock you away in some safe place until I figure out what's going on around here. That's the kind of complication I mean." He scowled as she shifted her body a little. "Am I too heavy on you?"

Casey shook her head. She wasn't sure how she should react to what Alex had said, but she was quite certain about her physical sensations. "You feel wonderful. I love the weight of you," she told him with unabashed frankness.

At a loss as to what the fuss was actually all about, Alex ventured one possibility. "There's no other woman in my life, Casey. Is that what's bothering you? Wondering?"

She hesitated, then decided there was no point pretending. "Maybe partly," she answered. "I didn't know whether . . . Of course, I didn't take the time to ask. And it's none of my business anyway."

"Don't be so civilized. It's your business. We've made it your business. Now, what's the rest?"

"The rest?" she asked, then remembered using the word *partly*. What was this penchant she'd developed for true confessions? She thought for a moment, then spoke decisively. "Okay, if you really want to know, it boils down to this: I don't like throwing any kind of monkey wrench into anyone's life in any way whatsoever, that's all."

That's all, Alex thought, realizing that Casey was far more leery of attachment than he'd ever been. Leery? She had barriers around her that made the Great Wall of China look like a picket fence.

"The thing is," she went on, absently tracing the cords of his neck with the sides of her thumbs, "I want you to know I understand that this . . . this encounter . . . isn't the beginning of something . . ."

"Complicated?" Alex said helpfully.

His irony was lost on Casey. "That's right," she said, her manner prim even as her fingers moved downward and began frolicking in his chest hair. "I know you don't have time for a woman in your life."

"True," Alex agreed, trying to be honest and sensible. "It's been said that my work is my mistress. If so, this company is definitely an expensive and demanding one that leaves me precious little to offer a lady."

"You offer plenty," Casey murmured, then did a quick backtrack. "But I'm not trying to take you away from her . . . it . . . whatever. It's just the opposite, come to think of it. There I was, being a dedicated servant to your newspaper-mistress, and you came along and dragged me away."

"I didn't drag you. I carried you."

"Semantics. The truth is, I've become more of a liability than an asset. You wouldn't hover over . . ." She paused, reflecting that she could choose her words more carefully. "You wouldn't worry about Ron the way you do about me. You've had to adjust your weekend plans because—"

"Because Ron's sick, and I wouldn't leave any new editor to handle everything alone no matter what my personal feelings were," Alex stated.

Casey eyed him dubiously, then nodded. "Okay. I'll buy that. But I don't want you worrying about me."

"Sorry, I can't help it, sweetheart. I guess it's considered bad form nowadays for a man to feel protective of his . . ." He stopped and cleared his throat, not certain just what he'd been about to say. Toward his what? His editor? Hardly. His squeeze? Not his style. His woman? Good grief, was that it? Was he beginning to think in phrases straight out of the country-and-western hit parade? Where Casey was concerned, was he turning into some kind of emotional redneck?

Yes.

It was time to get back to being sensible, he told himself. "Shouldn't allowances be made when the woman in question happens to be threatened because of things the man in question has done, problems he's created, controversies he's stirred up?" he reasoned.

"Your protective male instincts are all very fine, perhaps even . . . well, rather appealing," Casey answered cautiously. "But I'm not used to counting on anyone else's protection, and I've never learned to expect it. What's more, I don't care much for the terms it imposes."

"Terms?"

Casey heaved a deep sigh and braced himself for Alex's anger. "Okay, here goes. All that protectiveness is a kind of cage, rationalized by the best of motives, but still a cage. You're worried about me, so I have to do whatever you say—for my own good, of course. I can't go here or there, daren't do this or that, mustn't get involved in your troubles. Why? Because you'll worry. I can't handle my job properly if doing it gives you cause to worry. I have to turn in my key so you won't need to worry." She paused, then added softly, "I don't like cages, Alex. They give me claustrophobia."

Aware there was a great deal of truth in what Casey was saying—even more than she knew—Alex was nevertheless stung by her words. He told himself to roll off her and stop indulging in the worrying that seemed to offend her so much. Let her go on her merry way, he thought. Then he wouldn't have to try to figure her out.

But he couldn't move. In the midst of a no-win balance-of-power discussion, he was crushing this delectable woman under him with his superior strength and was clearly capable of making her want him with mindless passion, while she was demolishing his argument with her irrefutable logic and arousing a hunger in him that only she could appease. Maybe they were both a little nuts. "Like I said, I can't help it, sweetheart," he said huskily, struggling to hang onto his male prerogative to watch over the woman in his life. And like it or not, Casey had become the woman in his life. "I . . . need to know you're safe."

Casey knew she'd better score whatever point she

could before the debate was halted by powerful natural causes. The heat emanating from Alex was
setting her on fire, and her body was readying itself
for him with a will of its own. "What if I told you not
to go to Seattle because I was afraid something might
happen to you there?" she asked with shaky deter-
mination. "Would you skip the conference?"

"That's ridiculous," Alex said, sliding his hands
under Casey's body to lift her to him. "And it's
different."

"Is it?"

"Yes. Well, maybe not . . ." Alex glowered down at
her. His thinking processes were a little fuzzy. Casey
had parted her thighs so instinctively, she didn't
even seem aware of what was happening. "I don't
know," he muttered. "It sure as hell seems different to
me."

"Well, it's not," Casey stated flatly.

Yet in the very next second she no longer thought
about cages or complications or germs of panic. Alex
was plunging into her, driving everything from her
consciousness but her wild, primitive need for him.

The Friday morning pasteup went smoothly, and
Casey handed over the completed pages in plenty of
time to be proofread before they were picked up by
the printer's courier. Alex had helped, but not as
much as the previous week. Casey was buzzing with
pride at her growing expertise.

Marg did a quick perusal of the flats, then set them
aside for a closer look when her own pages were
caught up. "I hope there won't be any delivery problems this week," she said as she gave Casey several
ads to check over.

"There won't be," Casey said, returning to her

worktable. "Alex phoned some people in that business group of his to keep an eye on things. He's also done a little bartering with a friend who owns a security company—advertising space in return for a professional to patrol the area until our kids have finished their routes."

For the next several minutes Casey found herself smiling inwardly as Marg and Sandra launched into their inevitable recitation of Alex's endless virtues, the wonder in their voices sounding as if they were realizing for the very first time what a sainted genius he was.

The saint himself poked his head into the composing room. "Casey, may I see you in my office, please?" he said curtly, then disappeared.

Not again! she thought with plummeting spirits, vividly remembering how he'd summoned her the same way the previous week. Then it was her résumé that had set him off. What was it this time?

"Poor Alex," Marg murmured, frowning and shaking her head. "He's so harried these days."

Casey rolled her eyes and got to her feet. Poor Alex? What about poor Casey? Coping with that man was like riding a roller coaster. He hadn't seemed too harried during the night, she'd noticed. He hadn't been quite so cool when he'd awakened her in the sweetest way possible early that morning, or when he'd lured her into the shower with him. He'd been full of laughter and overflowing affection when he'd taken her home to change from her hopelessly wrinkled skirt and blouse to a yellow cotton shirtdress, and he'd been adorably charming at The Starting Gate, perfectly comfortable about the two of them joining Brittany for breakfast. Right until he'd gone into his office, satisfied that the pasteup was well under control, Alex had been in high spirits.

So what could have happened?

Then she remembered. The key. He really wanted her to turn in the damn key.

She grabbed her purse and dug out her key case, jangling it noisily and working the office key off the ring as she marched out of the room and across the hall.

Alex was standing in front of his desk when she strode into his office. She barely managed to shut the door rather than slam it behind her. Refusing to let herself be weakened by the unsettling memory of what his tall, lean body looked like under his dark blue business suit, she stalked over to him, snatched up his hand, and slapped the key down on his open palm. "There," she said. "Satisfied?"

He scowled down at the key for several seconds before he understood. He'd forgotten all about asking for it.

He took Casey's hand, pressed the key into her palm, and folded her fingers over it. "I changed my mind."

Casey was thoroughly confused. "So it's all right if I come in to work when no one's around?"

"No, but it was rotten of me to demand your key as a hostage. All I ask is a promise that you'll stay out of here until nine o'clock on Monday morning."

"My word's enough? Even though you've told me repeatedly to stay away after hours and I've come in anyway?"

Alex grinned, a silvery glint of amusement appearing in his eyes. "But I've never asked for your word. As you've pointed out in your own sweet way, I've been too busy giving orders—which you've never agreed to follow. I believe that once you do make a promise, Casey, you'll keep it."

She was dubious. Alex was being entirely too

reasonable. "What if something comes up that needs my attention?"

"It can wait, whatever it is. Let's face it, honey: We're running a neighborhood weekly here, not conducting a last-chance summit for world peace." Slightly surprised by his own attitude Alex realized that he was poking fun more at himself than at Casey. Until her well-being had become his paramount concern, he had allowed his newspaper chain to take on far too much importance. "Well?" he prompted as he realized Casey hadn't answered him yet. "Do I hear any sincere promises yet?"

After another moment of careful consideration Casey nodded. She couldn't think of any reason to work at the office over the weekend anyway. "Okay, it's a deal. Now, if you weren't after my key, why did you summon me in here in that *tone* of yours? I thought I was in hot water again."

Alex cocked his head to one side, his expression almost puzzled. "I didn't summon you in any *tone*. I asked if I could see you in my office. I even said please."

"You sounded angry. Forbidding. Downright mean."

"I did?"

Casey softened. Poor Alex. He honestly was surprised. Was it possible she was overly sensitive? Had she reverted to her old habit of looking for trouble as soon as someone got too close to her? If so, she must be a walking time bomb, because nobody, ever, had touched the deepest part of her being the way Alex had. "Well, maybe you just sounded . . . harried," she conceded, silently thanking Marg for the useful word.

"Or maybe it was something else entirely," Alex suggested with a disarming little grin.

"Such as?" she murmured, a telltale catch in her voice.

Alex curved his hands around her shoulders and drew her toward him. "Try . . . impatient."

"And impulsive?" Casey ventured.

Nodding he reached up to cradle her face between his hands. "And impetuous."

Desire clouded Casey's eyes, and a smile curved her lips as she melted against him, her arms around his waist.

"I have to leave for the airport in a few minutes," he said, the expression in his blue eyes hauntingly tender. "I need something from you before I go. Something important."

"What . . . what would that be?" Casey asked, though she had a fairly good idea.

"This, of course," Alex murmured as he dipped his head and covered her lips with his.

Casey was intoxicated instantly, her senses reeling from the minty sweetness of Alex's mouth, her imagination fired by the intimate thrusts of his tongue, her body aching to be joined with his again.

She was beginning to think her longing would be fulfilled right there on Alex's desk when he abruptly released her mouth, wrapped his arms around her, and held her with a fierce possessiveness that should have aroused all her old fears—but didn't. "Come to Seattle with me," he whispered, then gave a hoarse, startled laugh. "I warned you I was feeling impetuous, didn't I?"

Casey tipped back her head to look up at him with a quizzical smile. "What's happening with us, Alex?" she asked softly. "Are we moving a bit fast?"

He drew a deep breath and let it out slowly. "Maybe. Maybe too fast."

Their gazes locked for several long, charged seconds, as if they were trying to read the future in each other's eyes. Then, by an unspoken agreement, Alex relaxed his hold on Casey, and she moved out of the circle of his arms.

The tension in the room was thick. Casey moved to the window and stood looking out, her arms folded over her midriff.

Alex, going behind his desk to slide some papers into his briefcase, wasn't sure what to say or do at this point. He'd never been as far off balance in his life as he was with Casey.

"Thanks for the invitation," Casey said without turning to look at him. "The conference, I mean. Asking me to go with you was sweet."

Sweet, Alex thought. Sweetness had nothing to do with his motives. But it was a good tack to follow, so he said lightly, "I wish I'd suggested sooner that you could come along. How about it, though? There might still be time . . ."

"Alex, I happen to know you signed up for that conference weeks ago," Casey said, turning to smile at him. "And I honestly would prefer to hold down the fort here."

"Hold down the fort?" he repeated with an edge in his voice as he clicked his briefcase shut. "Casey, everything's under control for the deliveries, so there's no reason for you to give a thought to this paper for the next two days. It's a weekend, remember?"

"A weekend with Sea Festival events to cover and stories happening all over the West End," she pointed out. "Besides, we've been letting the most important thing slide: We still haven't tried to find out who owns that numbered real-estate company. I have a strong hunch your old friend Jimmy Dawson is in there somewhere like the proverbial dirty shirt. You've said yourself he's into all sorts of sleaze, and it doesn't get much sleazier than renting out a property to that tacky strip club. I'm sure I could find out—"

"Casey, don't find out anything," Alex cut in sharply. "Don't go near the See-More again. Don't—"

"But it's crucial!" Casey persisted, then barreled ahead, her words tumbling out in a rush. "I've been going through our back issues again, and they started me thinking. Wouldn't a developer like Dawson love to get his hands on this house—or more to the point, the land it's sitting on? If he could run *The Weekender* out of business, he'd be rid of the one person who's making things uncomfortable for him, *and* he'd be able to snatch up your property at a sacrifice! Pretty strong motives for a multipronged attack on your paper, wouldn't you say? I'm convinced that all your troubles lead straight back to Jimmy Dawson. I'll bet anything we'll find out he's tied in with *The Gazette* somehow—"

"Stop!"

Casey closed her mouth and scowled.

Alex strode across the room and planted his hands on Casey's shoulders. "No more digging, understand? Especially when I'm out of town! Okay, I agree with your hunch—all your hunches. As a matter of fact I already have someone looking into Dawson's unpublicized holdings. Someone who specializes in that kind of research. So you stay out of it, Strawberry. Just stay the hell out of it!"

"You agree with me?" she said with a sudden smile. Absently reaching up to straighten Alex's striped silk tie, she went on with excitement shimmering in her voice. "You have some kind of professional doing all that checking? That's wonderful! You didn't tell me."

That wasn't all he hadn't told her, Alex thought with a frisson of guilt. But he brushed it away. Casey had proved to him he'd done the right thing. "Sweet-heart, please understand: It's not that I'll actually be worrying . . ."

"Perish the thought," she drawled.

He narrowed his eyes and tightened his grip on her shoulders. "Okay, I admit it. I'll worry. I have a long way to go before I manage to curb that tendency. So humor me. Would you *try* to stay out of trouble?"

"For heaven's sake, what trouble could I get into?"

"I don't know. That's what worries me."

Casey stared at him for several seconds, then burst out laughing. "You win, Alex. I'll stick to interviewing the winners of the bathtub races and the barbecued-rib cook-offs. I'll stay away from the Dawson construction site, I won't go within three blocks of Club See-More, and . . ." She smiled sweetly. "Am I for-getting anything?"

"Don't go walking in the park after sunset," Alex answered without pausing to think. "And—" He stopped short as he saw Casey's eyebrows shooting up. "Eat an apple every day, get to bed by three," he said with a self-mocking grin, borrowing the words of a corny old song to show he understood how ridicu-lously fretful he was being. "My overprotectiveness is showing again?"

Casey laughed. "Yes. Now cut it out, will you?" *Please cut it out,* she added silently. *Please.* Because heaven help her, she was beginning to like the way it made her feel.

Nine

As Casey finished her presunset walk through Stanley Park, she wished she could relax and enjoy the perfect summer evening. But she was having trouble shaking the unnerving sensation that she was being followed by a large, balding man with a bulldog face, a barrel chest, and shoulders that shouldn't be allowed off a football field.

Perhaps Alex's constant nagging about her safety had made her more uneasy than usual, Casey reflected, heading along a street that would take her out of the park and onto the main drag right at The Starting Gate. After all, she'd wandered through the most-frequented areas of the giant nature preserve, so there was no real reason to wonder why The Bulldog kept turning up in the same general vicinities.

No matter, she told herself as she reached the diner. If the gentleman had been tailing her, she'd managed to lose him, and she'd enjoyed the little adventure. But why would anyone be trailing her in the first place?

"Hi, Ruby," she said as she went into the diner and slid onto her usual stool at the counter. She was the only customer; rush hour was over. "What's for supper? Did the starving hordes leave anything for me?"

"How about giving my chicken salad a try?"

"Sounds great," Casey answered cheerfully. "And maybe some iced tea with it?"

"Coming right up, kiddo." As she took a pitcher from the refrigerator and filled a glass, Ruby grinned over her shoulder at Casey. "Smiley was saying earlier today that we ought to put a brass plate on that stool with your name engraved on it. You come here more than Cookie does. Even more than Scoop. Personally, I figure we should adopt you." She laughed easily as she set the tea in front of Casey. "I wouldn't mind people thinking I could produce a daughter like you."

A huge lump suddenly formed in Casey's throat even though she knew the older woman was joking. "You've already adopted me," she managed to say, then picked up her frosty glass and tossed back a large gulp of the contents.

"Well, the hair matches," Ruby said, patting her own Lucy Ricardo–red curls. "Close enough, anyway." She went back to the fridge to take out the makings for Casey's chicken salad. "Did you get Scoop off to Seattle?"

"He left at lunchtime," Casey answered, still having trouble finding her voice and feeling ridiculous about getting so emotional. Her infernal craving to *belong*, she thought with a shaft of impatience. Would it always be at odds with her need for independence?

She was beginning to realize that something, someday, would have to give.

Pulling herself together she asked brightly, "Where's the love of your life this evening?"

"Married to Joanne Woodward, last I heard," Ruby

shot back, then relented immediately, as if she couldn't even kid about being disloyal to her Smiley. "Truth is, His Nibs is in the back kitchen taking care of a few repairs."

"I can't fathom you two," Casey said with a shake of her head. "You're always, always on duty. Don't you get tired?"

"Of what? Of fixing good meals for nice people? Of visiting friends all day long and calling it work?"

"Well . . . of each other?" Casey asked timidly, not sure why she would ask such a personal question. When she was conducting interviews, she was bold. Socially she was the opposite.

"Of each other?" Ruby echoed, then chortled as she went on chopping onion and celery and various other ingredients. "You have to understand, Strawberry. Smiley and me, we're a team. And when you're a team, you don't get tired of each other. It'd be like getting tired of yourself." She stopped, her knife suspended in midair. "Come to think of it, I'm more inclined to get tired of myself than of Smiley. He doesn't yak-yak-yak all the time like I do."

Casey laughed and protested that being an interesting conversationalist was not yakking, then lapsed into thoughtful silence as Ruby shrugged and finished chopping.

"Speaking of teams," Ruby said a few moments later, "I was glad to see Scoop come in here with you this morning. You two are good together. That kind of thing shows, you know what I mean? And listen, after the number he let that little me-first JoBeth do on him, it's high time he found a girl smart enough to appreciate a great guy when she finds one."

Good lord, Casey thought, couldn't anything be kept private in this neighborhood? She decided firmly and unequivocally not to encourage Ruby's gossip.

Ruby worked on in complacent silence, humming to herself as she prepared Casey's salad with a toss of her special yogurt-based dressing and arranged the mixture attractively on a bed of crisp leaf lettuce.

"There you go," she said when she proudly placed it in front of Casey.

"Looks wonderful," Casey said, tucking into the dish immediately. "Tastes fabulous," she added dutifully but truthfully after her first sample. She settled in to enjoy the cozy feeling Ruby's delicious food and good-natured mothering always gave her.

By the time she'd let Ruby talk her into trying a raspberry tart for dessert, Casey was an utterly contented woman, not missing Alex at all. Not giving him more than a moment's thought. Not the least bit curious to find out what Ruby knew about the woman who'd once shared his life. His name. His bed . . .

It was with some surprise, therefore, that she heard a voice very much like her own saying casually, "So, Ruby. You knew this JoBeth person Alex was married to?"

Three-quarters of an hour later, bristling with indignation, Casey heaped compliments on Ruby for the greatest chicken salad ever concocted and left the diner with a friendly wave of her hand and murder in her heart.

Preoccupied with the rank injustices Alex had put up with because of his ridiculously overdeveloped sense of responsibility and misplaced guilt—allowing JoBeth to take him for every cent, only to see her run off right after the divorce with an unpleasant but filthy-rich heir to old San Francisco money—Casey almost didn't notice The Bulldog sitting at a sidewalk café right across the street.

By Saturday evening Casey still couldn't shake the feeling she was being watched and followed, though she hadn't seen her shadow since her eyes had met his in one brief moment of shock outside The Starting Gate.

But she'd spent most of the day in the midst of the Sea Festival mobs, concentrating on collecting off-beat stories and snapshots that could be used for *The Weekender*'s coverage of the annual superparty, so it was entirely possible her nemesis had been dogging her heels without her seeing him.

Unless, she reminded herself, it was all her imagination.

She began to relax when, after staying out late to watch the fireworks over English Bay, she walked home alone and made it without incident.

Imagination, she decided. Probably The Bulldog was a retired florist who enjoyed a daily stroll through the park. She put him out of her mind so completely, she didn't even mention him when Alex thrilled her with a call from Seattle late that night.

After pulling on sneakers, jeans, and a Save the Dolphins T-shirt on Sunday morning, Casey went to Stanley Park to cover a band concert, an ethnic dancing display, and several amateur sports events. Later she wandered over to The Somerset Inn, where Brittany, as manager of the small luxury hotel, was playing host to the Hospitality Games as well as being a good sport herself: She was taking part enthusiastically in the bed-making races, find-the-lost-luggage contests, and whatever else the bent minds of Lotus Land had thought up for the sake of a few laughs at the expense of the travel and hotel industry.

When the games ended, Casey and Brittany had dinner together, then walked home after dusk, parting company as Britt headed for her apartment a couple of streets north of Casey's.

Casey was half a block from her building when the car pulled up to hug the curb beside her, its driver slowing his pace to match her purposeful gait.

This time it definitely was not her imagination.

The low-slung black Corvette was a sixties classic Casey would love to have taken a long, appreciative look at under other circumstances. As it was, she felt like a deer being tracked by a hungry cougar. She watched it from the corner of her eye.

It was some creep looking for a pickup, she told herself as she strode blithely along, pretending not to notice her unwelcome escort. But she was glad she'd worn her shoulder bag with the strap across her body, leaving her hands free.

Suddenly the car sprinted ahead, then slammed to a halt a few yards in front of Casey. The door opened, and a weight-lifting-class graduate in tight jeans and a muscle shirt unfolded himself from the bucket seat. He stretched to a feet-astride position in Casey's path, facing her with a lazy grin. He took his time reading the message on her T-shirt, then shook his head and snorted. "I knew when I saw that mop of blond hair that this was my lucky night."

Casey had stopped in her tracks. There was no sense trying to breeze on by. This character smelled like a distillery and was looking for trouble. "A guy who has the moxie to own a 'Vette ought to be bright enough to treat it better," she said with outward calm, hoping her comment would throw him off enough to give her a few seconds to think. He seemed familiar, but she couldn't place him.

He was thrown off by her remark for an instant. Not long enough, though. His grin returned, "I know how to treat my car, gorgeous. Just like I know how to treat a woman."

"Good for you. Now let's see if you know how to get out of my way, Galahad."

"The name's not Galahad. It's Marty. And maybe I don't want to get out of your way, pretty lady. Maybe I want you to climb into my 'Vette and come with me. Someplace more private, say. What're you gonna do about that?"

Casey hoped he couldn't see her heart pounding or her knees quaking. Showing her fear wouldn't help. "What am I going to do about it?" she asked with a show of indifference. "I'll come up with something, sweetcakes. Count on not liking it." She raked him with the most scathing gaze she could muster. "Why don't you step to one side like a good boy and save yourself a lot of trouble?"

His grin disappeared, and a flicker of doubt flared up in his eyes before he threw back his head and hooted with laughter.

That instant of unsureness was Casey's clue. "You're one of Vic Lundstrom's big, brave hard hats," she said, then felt sheer rage lance through her. "Why, you've been following me all weekend, you—"

"Whaddya talking about?" he cut in, looking offended. "I spotted you ten minutes ago out on the main street, figured I oughta catch up and earn myself a bonus by teaching McLean's girl some manners."

"Teaching me some manners?" Casey repeated, rolling her eyes derisively even though she was barely controlling the tremor in her voice. Bravado seemed like her best chance to get out of this mess. "Why do boors always think they can teach somebody else manners? By the way, are you hiding the rest of the crew under a rock nearby? I know you wouldn't be this brave all by yourself."

Marty let out a long, low whistle. "Honey, you are really asking for it. And I'm just the man to give it to you." He grinned again, then pounced, closing his large hand around her left arm.

Casey's reaction was lightning fast and instinctive, though not precisely what she'd been taught in the self-defense class she'd taken a few years before: She slugged him. Her fisted right hand smashed into his face above the bridge of his nose.

Caught by surprise he yowled and let go of her arm, staggering back with both hands clapped over his forehead.

Deciding not to hang around for a brawl she wasn't likely to win in the long run, Casey took off and hoped Marty was too stunned and drunk to pursue her. But he recovered fast, catching up and grabbing her arm again before she'd gone five steps. She whirled and caught him in one knee with a kung-fu kick. But Marty wouldn't give up. His meaty paw closed over her shoulder, digging into her flesh and yanking her back so she couldn't kick again. "Let me *go*!" she yelled, realizing belatedly she should have been screaming for help all along. Lifting her foot and positioning it over his, she was set to stomp down hard and then battle with whatever strength and resources she could dredge up. There was a time to run and a time to fight.

Hearing footsteps she craned her neck and looked back to see if some policeman had heard her yell.

She froze. The Bulldog! Oh lord, now she'd had it.

So much for staying out of trouble. Alex was going to be furious!

But the vicious grip on her shoulder loosened, and she pitched forward. Scrambling to regain her balance and turn at the same time, she saw The Bulldog gathering the back of her attacker's shirt and twisting the grimacing hard hat's arm behind his back.

Casey's jaw dropped.

"Sorry, miss," The Bulldog said with a regretful smile. "I didn't like to interfere, seeing as how you seemed to have everything under control, but I've got my orders."

Casey was at her worktable on Monday afternoon, blue-penciling press releases and lying in wait for Alex.

He breezed in just after four, all smiles for everyone and warm, secret glances for Casey.

The instant he'd finished answering a barrage of questions from Marg and Sandra about the conference, Casey got to her feet and said abruptly, "Alex, may I see you in your office, please?"

"Of course," Alex answered, suppressing a delighted grin as he eagerly led the way. She was so damn cute, he thought with a rush of mingled desire and affection. So playfully sexy. Obviously she was turning the tables on him, summoning him into his office for a stolen kiss the way he'd done with her on Friday. She was an irresistible, adorable minx, captivatingly lovely in a coral silk blouse and cream-colored slacks, her hair caught up in a loosely cascading Bardot style he hadn't seen on her before. He liked the look. He could hardly wait to take down every soft curl and wayward tendril. His fingers tingled with eagerness for the feel of those silky strands rippling over them.

Opening his office door, Alex stepped back to let Casey go in ahead of him. She marched across the room over to his desk and turned to face him, her hands on her hips.

She was playing her role to the hilt, Alex thought as he closed the door and went to her, inhaling her sweet fragrance and longing for the delicious nectar of her mouth.

He was about to draw her into his arms when Casey reached up with both hands and grabbed him by the lapels. "You put a detective on me!" she said furiously. "You hired somebody to follow me from the minute you left town on Friday afternoon!"

"I didn't hire him. He happens to be the head of the security company that's investigating our hunches about Dawson and was keeping tabs on our delivery routes. All I did was ask him to keep an eye on you as well." Alex had been hoping Casey wouldn't find out what he'd done, but he wasn't going to deny it. "Anyway, how do you know about all this? And when did you realize it?"

"On Friday afternoon. *Early* Friday afternoon," Casey said with a touch of triumph in her tone.

Alex's brows arched with surprise. "So soon?"

"I'm a reporter, remember? A trained observer, as they say." Casey let go of Alex's lapels and turned her back on him, folding her arms over her waist. "So much for my word being enough for you. So much for trusting me to keep my promise." She whirled to face him again, jabbing her index finger into his chest. "After everything we've . . . after all the . . . you *still* don't trust me!"

"Casey McIntyre, after everything that's happened between us," Alex countered quietly, catching her hand to stop her before she poked a hole through him, "how could you jump to such a damn-fool conclusion? Trust had nothing to do with the situation. I couldn't be around to watch over you, so I made sure someone else was. I didn't tell you because I figured you'd take offense and do everything in your considerable power to lose him—which would defeat the purpose, wouldn't you agree?"

"I can't believe this," she muttered, trying in vain to retrieve her hand. "You actually had me . . ." Her mouth stayed open in midsentence as Alex's words finally worked their way past her outrage to her brain. "Watch over me?"

Alex brought her hand up to his lips and kissed the tips of her fingers. "To make sure you were safe, honey."

Determined not to be softened, Casey eyed him warily. "Why didn't The Bulldog tell me that? Why did he just make a cryptic comment about how he had his orders?"

"The Bulldog?"

"Your detective. He didn't tell me his name. He didn't tell me anything much, except that if I had questions, I should go to you with them."

"His name's Cecil Waters," Alex said, his lips twitching with amusement. He moved to perch on the corner of his desk, tugging Casey toward him. Letting go of her hands he splayed his long fingers over the sides of her slender waist. "Bulldog suits him better, I must admit. Smiley would be proud of you for coming up with such a perfect nickname. Now what do you mean, Cec didn't tell you anything? You actually talked to him?"

"Last night," Casey said. She wished she could control her body's instinctive response as Alex's taut thigh pressed against her flank. She'd rested her palms on his upper arms, fully intending to push herself away from him. But she could feel the strength and virility in the play of muscles under his dark suit, and somehow she found herself staying right where she was. How was she supposed to give Alex the dressing-down he deserved, she thought helplessly, when what she really wanted was to *un*dress him? "I'll have you know your Cecil Waters made a nervous wreck of me all weekend," she said with a thrust of her chin. "How was I supposed to know he was on our side?"

"I'm sorry, honey. But you weren't supposed to know about him at all. I can't get over the fact that Cec was clumsy enough to let you spot him right off the bat."

Alex's remark stirred a spark of pride in Casey. "He told me it's never happened to him before. And for the record, I sensed a presence all day Saturday and Sunday, and I know now your man was right there the whole time, but I didn't spot him once after Friday. He's good at his job, Alex. Don't give him a hard time when you get his report."

Alex coughed to cover a burst of laughter he couldn't quite suppress. Casey never ceased to catch him off guard. Even when she was angry, she was scrupulously fair. "Okay, I'll go easy on the guy," he promised. "How did you finally nail him last night?"

"I didn't—" Casey stopped short, frowning. Uh-oh, she thought. Now she would have to confess that The Bulldog had rescued her. She'd boxed herself in. Including, she realized as she instinctively took a step back, physically.

Alex responded by sliding his arms all the way around her waist and pulling her closer, trapping her hips between his strong thighs. "Don't go away," he said softly. "I've missed you, Strawberry. I want you right here where I can look at you and touch you and breathe you in."

Casey melted. "Oh Alex," she said with a sigh, her fingers sliding up to his shoulders, lightly trailing over his neck above his collar, then thrusting into his hair as she brought his mouth to hers. "I missed you too."

Countless explosions were going off inside Alex. He moved his hands over Casey's yielding body, wanting to touch her everywhere at once. As he recognized the beginnings of her eager surrender, he knew again the rush of exhilaration and raw male triumph Casey inspired. And for the first time since the plane had landed in Vancouver—the first time in more years than he could count—he felt he had come home.

As their kisses deepened, their mutual desire made a sharp ascent into regions much too dizzying for the time and place. With a great effort Alex ended the kiss. He stood and simply held Casey, their heart-beats drumming out a syncopated duet. "As we were discussing before you attacked me in your own inimitable way," he said with a raspy laugh, "how did you get talking to The Bulldog?"

It took Casey a moment to focus her thoughts, and even when she did, she hesitated a little longer, not at all eager to let Alex know how justified his protec-tiveness had been. But he was going to find out all the details anyway, so she met his mildly curious gaze head-on. "Okay, I have to admit that your watchdog—"

"Bulldog," Alex said with a grin. He was proud of Casey for having spotted Waters right away. He wanted to hear all the details. "What do you have to admit?"

"That Bulldog did happen along at an opportune

moment," she answered, then added hastily, "but even he said I already had things under control."

Alex's smile faded. "Had *what* under control?"

Casey winced and heaved a deep sigh, then told him how she'd been confronted, just as he'd predicted, by a drunk and threatening member of Vic Lundstom's crew. She didn't mention that she'd been foolish enough to trade insults with a man who outweighed her by about half a ton, and she put off telling Alex that she'd fought back instead of thinking to scream for help, but she let him know what Marty had said about earning a bonus from his boss for getting to her.

Alex's arms tightened around her like iron bands. "And you came in here to tear a strip off me for hiring Waters to protect you?" he asked in a tone that sent a shiver through her. "If Cec hadn't been on the scene, you could've been . . ." He blanched, then abruptly let Casey go, turned on his heel, and headed for the door.

"So now *you're* mad at *me*?" Casey demanded. "You didn't tell me a thing, and you expect me not to be upset?"

Putting his hand on the doorknob Alex turned to look at her. "I'm not mad at you, Casey."

"No? You ought to see the look in your eyes right now, Alex McLean. And where are you off to, anyway? We're in the middle of a discussion."

"No, we're not," Alex said through clenched teeth as he yanked open the door. "Our discussion is over for the moment. Right now I have more pressing matters to deal with."

Casey tore after him. "Wait for me. I'm going with you, wherever it is you're headed."

He whirled to curve his fingers around her arms and walked her backward until she was in his office, sitting in his chair, and staring up at him in shock. "You're not going anywhere, and if I have to tie you to this chair to make sure you'll stay put for once, I will."

Casey had the distinct feeling he meant it.

As he turned to leave, she muttered, "When are you going to accept the fact that I can fight my own battles?"

He paused to face her one more time. "Casey, I do accept it. You, however, are so busy nursing your precious independence, you're overlooking a crucial detail: You weren't fighting your own battles last night. You were fighting mine. And you, of all people, should understand why that's a situation I won't tolerate."

After shouldering his way past a protesting secu- rity guard outside James O. Dawson's penthouse office suite overlooking English Bay, Alex refused to be waylaid by a startled receptionist or the sputtering secretary who tried to keep him out of Dawson's inner sanctum.

Dawson was swiveling in a high-backed leather chair behind a chrome-and-smoked-glass table that had nothing on it but a crystal ash tray and the state-of-the-art telephone he was using. He looked up to see what the commotion was, waved his secretary away, and ended his call. "McLean, unless you're here to talk about printing a whole pile of retractions," he said without preamble, "get out."

Alex flattened his palms on the glass and leaned over the table that looked to him like some mediocre Hollywood set designer's idea of a business mogul's desk. The whole office looked that way. So did Daw- son, for that matter. He even had the requisite cigar stuck into the side of his mouth.

Dawson raised one bushy brow and stared pointedly at Alex's hands. "My secretary just polished that glass."

"Then you won't want me to ram your head through it," Alex spat out. "I'll say this once, Jimmy. Keep our battle between us. Tell your goons to stay away from my people. Kids and women are especially off limits, understand?"

"No, I don't understand. I don't know what you're talking about," Dawson said, then smirked. "And I can't be held responsible if a guy on one of my construction crews is bugged by some female's interference in his business."

Alex's temper snapped. He reached across the desk, grabbed the weasel by his hand-painted tie and silk shirt front, and hauled Dawson half out of his chair. "Maybe what you need, Jimmy, is a little encouragement to *feel* responsible for . . ." Suddenly he stopped. There was fear in Dawson's flat gray eyes, but there was a strange glint there as well. A satisfied gleam.

Dammit, Alex thought. He wanted to hit somebody. He especially wanted to hit Jimmy Dawson. He thought about what could have happened to Casey, and he wanted to use Jimmy Dawson to repolish the pretentious desk. But it was a sucker's play, and Alex knew it. The last thing he needed was to make Dawson look like a victim, to give him an excuse to press charges for common assault and launch a lawsuit. "Jimmy," he said at last, his voice a menacing whisper, "there's nothing I'd like better than to rearrange your face, but I'd be doing you too many favors if I did." Shoving Dawson back into his chair and releasing him, Alex balled his hands into fists at his sides. "You're on the way out, Jimmy. Out of business and out of town. And that's a promise."

"Funny, I was thinking the same about you," Dawson shot back.

"We'll see," Alex said, turning to go. As he reached the door, he looked back with a cold glare. "By the way, take responsibility, Jimmy. Tell your hired help to stay away from the lady. Because if anybody goes near her again, I give you my word: I'll come back here, and I'll hurt you."

Ten

Alex was halfway to the Dawson construction site, the adrenaline still pumping through him and his blood still boiling, when Cecil Waters pulled up in his blue Buick and leaned across the passenger seat to push open the door.

Alex climbed into the car. "Are you following *me* now, Cec?"

The big man grinned. "Bulldog. Strawberry calls me Bulldog. I like it."

Alex rolled his eyes and raked his fingers through his hair. "I understand you two hardly talked. What's with the nicknames?"

"We talked some. I just didn't give her any of the details I figured you'd want to fill in."

"How'd you happen to come along now?" Alex asked, clenching and unclenching his hands, impatient to get where he was going and wade into a satisfying brawl. "Strawberry phoned you, right?"

"She said you'd be either at Dawson's throat or over at the project site taking on a whole construction crew."

Alex nodded. He might have known Casey couldn't sit still and keep out of things. Well, at least this time she'd been sensible enough to call in professional help. "She was right. I saw Dawson and had my say."

"You didn't hit him, did you?"

Alex shook his head. "I settled for giving him a warning."

"And now?"

Alex's eyes narrowed as he stared straight ahead. "Now I've got a score to settle at that project site. I don't like thugs threatening a lady—especially when it's because of a quarrel with me."

"Can't say I blame you, Alex. Go for the nose, though. Or knock out some teeth. The guy already has two black eyes."

Alex looked sharply at the detective. "You pasted him? Good. I owe you for that."

Bulldog chuckled quietly, his barrel chest heaving. "No, you owe Strawberry."

"Strawberry . . . ?"

"Man, she landed a sweet punch," Bulldog said with obvious relish. "Right between the eyes. The kind where the bruises spread until a guy looks like a raccoon. I stepped in to save him, not her."

Alex blinked once, then exploded with laughter. "That woman is more than any man can handle," he said with a shake of his head when he'd settled down.

"So do you still want to take on that construction crew?" Bulldog asked. "If you do, I'm with you. But why bother? The punk you're after isn't there anyway. He was a mean, stupid drunk looking for trouble. When he saw your girl, he figured he could score points with Dawson by roughing her up a little. I poured him into his car and drove him home, and earlier today I dropped by to ask him a few questions. Didn't get much, but he won't be bothering Strawberry again. For one thing he figures he owes her because she didn't turn him in to the cops."

After thinking things over Alex nodded. The way he'd been acting for the past little while, he wasn't much better than the swaggering young drunk. "You're right, Cec. I'll skip the brawling and go back to the office. How about a quick verbal report on the way?"

As Waters told him everything he'd found out so far, Alex wasn't surprised that all his suspicions—and Casey's—were confirmed. *The Gazette* and the numbered real-estate firm were Dawson holdings. So were several prime properties on both sides of Alex's house. There were plenty of reasons besides a few fiery newspaper editorials for Jimmy Dawson to want *The Weekender* put out of business. "But do we have anything solid?" Alex asked when Waters had finished. "Anything that could prove there are kick-backs and strong-arm tactics and everything else we know about?"

"Not yet," the detective admitted. "But stay cool, okay? We'll get this guy, but you've got to have a little patience. Let us keep digging up dirt on Jimmy Dawson while you plug away at what you do best: running your papers and stirring up trouble." Bull-dog grinned again as he pulled up in front of *The Weekender* to drop Alex off. "Now that you're back in town, I'm turning in my guardian-angel wings. Strawberry wore me out. She's all yours from here on in."

Remembering his furious threat to tie Casey to a chair, Alex sighed. All his? Right now he wasn't so sure.

• • •

Casey was in a quandary as she puttered at useless tasks in the composing room, constantly darting nervous glances at her watch.

It was just after five. Alex wasn't back yet, and everyone else had left. Casey didn't want to break her promise about not staying alone at the office, yet she couldn't bring herself to leave until she was certain he was all right. Visions of Alex taking on Vic Lundstrom and his entire crew had been tormenting her since he'd stormed out. She only hoped her call to Bulldog had done some good.

When she heard a key grating in the front-door lock, she flew out to the hall, then stopped short and braced herself, praying Alex hadn't been pulverized beyond repair.

"Alex," she said softly when he opened the door and stepped inside. He was fine. No black eyes, no missing teeth, no blood. He hadn't even wrinkled his suit. "Oh Alex, thank heavens!" Rushing to him she threw her arms around his neck and showered his puzzled face with kisses.

Astounded by the greeting, Alex's reaction was slow and awkward, his hands groping the air before coming to rest lightly on Casey's waist.

She felt tears slipping from the corners of her eyes, and for once she didn't try to stop them. "I shouldn't have blurted out everything about that silly fiasco last night without stopping to think how you'd react," she said, her voice thick with emotion. "And it was horrible of me to jump on you the minute you got back, all because of my wounded pride. My stupid, everlasting pride. I didn't want to admit that you were right, or that I was glad Bulldog was around when I needed him. So what did I do? I talked myself into an unreasonable snit. Isn't it ironic? Just the other day I said I didn't want to cause any complications for you, yet I made such a hash of things, you could have been beaten up or . . ."

"But I wasn't," Alex said gently, wrapping his arms around her and holding her close. "C'mon, baby, don't be upset. Everything's fine." He had no idea what to make of this turn of events. He'd been ready to face Casey's simmering anger, or her intense curiosity about what he'd been doing, or her put-me-in-coach eagerness to rejoin the battle after having been benched for a while, but her reaction threw him. If he'd gained some sort of advantage in his ongoing tussle with Casey, it was a hollow victory. A contrite Casey wasn't his Casey. He wanted his Casey back. Dropping a kiss to the tip of her nose, he grinned down at her. "Hey, you don't think I went out spoiling for a fight, do you?" he said in the most appalled tone he could pull off. "A *physical* one? You can't believe for a minute I'd do a thing like that!"

Casey might have bought his act if it weren't so patently phony. Besides, she'd seen him in action— she knew better. "I don't think it, I know it," she said, a smile tugging at her lips. It faded in the next moment as she cradled his face between her palms and searched his eyes, speaking earnestly and beseechingly. "Alex, I went out of my mind wondering what was happening. I can't bear that sort of thing. If there's trouble, I need to be there with you, on your side, doing whatever I can. I'm not the waiting-in-the-wings type. Please don't ever ask it of me again."

"Ever?" he repeated softly.

Casey stiffened, and a scarlet flush suffused her cheeks. "I mean . . . while all this mess is going on," she said hastily, lowering her hands to his chest and staring fixedly at the cleft of his chin. "I wasn't trying

to suggest that we're . . . that I . . ." Her words
trailed off as she realized she was going from bad to
worse.

"To suggest what?" Alex prompted, surprised to
find how much he was enjoying Casey's blunders.

Casey tried to extricate herself from his arms, but
he didn't choose to let her go. As she'd discovered
long before, when Alex didn't choose to let her go, she
stayed where she was. "It was a figure of speech," she
muttered. "And a foolish one at that. It's not your
problem if I go crazy with worry when you take off on
some kind of search-and-destroy mission the way
you did a while ago."

"Worry?" he said, deciding he could and should
score a point or two after all. "You *worry* about me,
Casey? But you don't believe in that sort of thing, do
you?" Touching his lips to her cheek, he tasted her
tears and was moved, but he made himself forge
ahead. "I seem to recall a little talk we had about
cages. Something to the effect that one person's
worrying restricts the other's freedom?"

"You have no shame," Casey grumbled. "How could
you bring up that discussion now, when I'm merely
trying to apologize and explain . . . ?"

"It seems fairly relevant," he answered cheerfully.
"And I'd just as soon you'd quit apologizing and
explaining. You really have nothing to apologize for,
all right? You know what I think we both need? A
night off. A few hours of forgetting all these stupid
problems and enjoying ourselves." When he saw
Casey's eyes widen with the beginnings of a protest,
Alex quickly added, "Don't worry, honey, I'll give you
a quick update on everything I know at this point
about what Jimmy Dawson's up to—most of which
you've figured out on your own. But afterward let's
not have any more shoptalk. We'll have dinner some-

where, and then . . . well, let's see what develops. How does that sound?"

Casey pretended to think it over. "I could probably cope," she answered after a good five seconds. "Do you like spaghetti?"

"Doesn't everybody?" Alex said, his arms tightening around her as a wave of emotion suddenly swept over him—an emotion he was almost ready to name. "Is there any particular Italian place you'd like to go to?"

"Yes. Casa Casey," she answered with a laugh. "One of the surrogate mothers I adopted when I was a kid was a fabulous lady from Napoli. She taught me her own sauce recipe, and I've had it simmering in my slow cooker since this morning, hoping some travel-weary publisher might like a home-cooked meal."

Alex gave her a quizzical smile. "Weren't you angry at me as of this morning?"

"Actually I was fantasizing about wringing your neck," Casey admitted unhesitatingly.

"Yet you intended to invite me to your apartment for spaghetti?"

"Sure. Why wouldn't I? Being angry about some little thing doesn't mean not . . ." Casey almost bit off the end of her tongue as she clamped her mouth shut, realizing with a shock what she'd almost said.

"Not what?" Alex said, his pulse leaping to a wild tarantella.

Casey didn't answer. She couldn't confess to Alex what she hadn't admitted to herself.

"Not what?" he persisted.

"Being angry doesn't mean not wanting to have dinner with a person," Casey said, then pulled herself together and smiled blandly. "Now, why don't you go change into something more comfortable while I close down the office for the night?"

Alex nodded, planted a chaste kiss on Casey's forehead, and headed upstairs to his apartment. As he stripped off his clothes and indulged in a quick shower, then pulled on white cotton slacks and a yellow polo shirt, he brooded about why he'd been so determined to make Casey finish her sentence—and why she'd refused to give him an honest answer.

They were quite a pair, he mused. Proud and independent? Or just scared and haunted by past hurts, past failures, past mistakes?

What they needed was time. Time for Casey to realize that she was a joy and an enrichment—not a complication—to any life she touched, especially his. Time for both of them to learn the tricky art of give-and-take. Time for him to grasp the incredible possibility that Casey's caring, like her loyalty, was the Old Man River of emotion: No matter what might happen, whether his whole existence came crashing down around him, whether he made decisions that outraged her, whether he infuriated or delighted her, it would just keep rolling along.

Time, Alex discovered to his pleased surprise over the next few weeks, was exactly what he and Casey were given.

Ron Coulter's recovery brought him back to work, cutting the day-to-day pressure down to a fraction of what it had been.

Jimmy Dawson seemed to have run out of dirty tricks or had decided too many of them had back-fired. The salesmen from *The Gazette* started playing it straight with advertisers, trying to regain the credibility they'd lost. There were no problems with delivery routes. With the help of Smiley, a pair of apologetic MBA students, and Alex's banker, the rumors of *The Weekender*'s looming demise died a quick and natural death.

"It's too quiet out there, boss," Casey said one evening as they stood side by side in Alex's large kitchen preparing steaks and potatoes to put on a barbecue he'd bought for the backyard. "Jimmy Dawson has to be up to something. Even Bulldog thinks so, though he hasn't been able to nail down anything solid."

"I agree," Alex said, then frowned. He put down the pastry brush he was using to coat the steaks with his special barbecue sauce, crooked his finger under Casey's chin, and tilted her head back so he could give her a stern look. "But would you quit calling me that?"

"Calling you boss?" Casey said with wide-eyed innocence. "But it's my privilege. "You *are* the boss."

Alex gave a derisive snort. "Sure. Now cut it out. It really bugs me, and you know it. Especially after working hours. Even during working hours, come to think of it. My two biggest fans in the composing room have taken to shooting disapproving glances my way whenever you use that word. They seem to think I must be Mr. Nice Guy in public and Attila the Hun in private."

"Okay, if that's the way you want it," Casey said, smiling sweetly. "After all you are the bo—"

Her sassy teasing was lost in the hot recesses of Alex's mouth, and within moments she'd have called him anything he wished. Their steak dinner, like so many others they'd shared, was a late one.

Gradually Casey began to open up to Alex, and he to her.

When they got around to talking about his divorce,

Casey surprised herself by asking outright why he'd allowed himself to be taken to the cleaners.

"Selfishness, basically," he said, then laughed as he saw Casey's instantly outraged expression. "Wait, Casey. Let me explain. I'd married JoBeth in good faith, thinking it was forever, but I didn't make her happy. Simple as that. And I wasn't happy either, so when she said she wanted out, I felt terrible but I was relieved. Giving JoBeth the keys to the candy store was a way to handle my guilt. Besides, I didn't need a time-consuming, unpleasant court battle that would end up with the lawyers getting the lion's share. Why not let JoBeth have it? Believe me, I signed everything over to her for my sake, not hers."

"I see what you mean," Casey said. "In your place I suppose I'd have done the same thing. And I'd have felt just as guilty about being glad to be out of the situation." She went on to tell Alex about her engagement, and the relief she'd felt when it had ended.

It occurred to her that her panicky feelings about getting deeply involved with a man seemed to have receded considerably.

Lying at night in the haven of Alex's arms, her naked body curled into his, Casey found it easy to talk to him, confide in him, reveal her deepest secrets and fears to him.

She told him, in one particularly unguarded moment, how she'd always panicked if any man inched too close. "A couple of years ago," she said with a slightly annoyed frown, "one rather pushy character called me a waltz-away lover—I took exception to that, since we weren't lovers, and I wasn't waltzing away, I was flat-out running from him. But there was some truth in the basic accusation, I suppose."

Alex laughed and hugged her close. "Sweetheart,

you were just saving the last waltz for the guy who was going to take you home."

Casey found herself doing a lot of thinking over the next few days about that remark.

As Alex felt Casey's confidence in him growing, he probed gently, gradually learning who she was, how she felt, why she'd been a "waltz-away lover." He suspected her emotional reserve was rooted in her conviction that she'd been an accident to her parents. But he kept wondering where she'd picked up such an idea. Had someone said it to her? Finally he felt he could ask. And he did.

Casey gave him a rueful little smile. "You know the old saw about eavesdroppers deserving what they hear about themselves? I learned it early—at about age seven, the first time I hid at the top of the stairs and heard my parents quarreling about whose fault it was that they'd been saddled with a baby. At the start I thought they meant I was about to get a little sister or brother, and I was thrilled. It made me feel guilty, considering that the folks didn't seem to want this child, but I couldn't help it. I started hugging myself with excitement, pretending I was hugging the—" Casey stopped, deciding there was no need to get maudlin, then went on. "The truth eventually dawned that it was me they were talking about. I was the baby they hadn't wanted. It was a bit of a shock, but it explained a certain stiltedness in any affection I'd felt from them."

The matter-of-fact understatement wrenched Alex's heart. He closed his eyes and tightened his arms around Casey—and around that little girl on the landing. "Sweetheart," he murmured huskily. "Parents are just tall kids trying to grow into responsibilities nobody's ever ready for. They didn't mean what they said."

"Yes, they did," Casey stated, then pressed a kiss to the underside of Alex's jaw as if to comfort him. He was upset about things she'd come to terms with long ago. "They meant it then, and they meant it every time they said it during later battles. I didn't and don't blame them for their bitterness, Alex. They'd started out as foreign correspondents and ended as teachers. My birth had shattered so many of their hopes, destroyed their dreams. . . ."

"Life has a way of making all of us adjust our dreams as we go along," Alex protested. He refused to keep silent in the face of her apparent guilt for having been born.

"I know," Casey answered. "And after all, they could have chosen not to have me, or keep me, or do their best to give me a stable home. I love my mother and father, and I know they love me in their way. But I never felt their home was mine, so I concentrated all my efforts on becoming self-sufficient as soon as possible." She propped herself up on one elbow and smiled down at him. "And I had all those surrogate families I've mentioned: Brittany's, the Italian people down the street, and my grandmother, until she died five years ago. In a lot of ways I was a very lucky kid." She nestled back down onto his broad chest and let her fingers indulge in the ever-fascinating exploration of the magnificent male body she was coming to know so intimately. With a soft laugh she added, "And right at this moment I'm feeling like the luckiest kid ever born."

Alex knew she'd talked as much as she wanted to—and besides, she was presenting him with an irresistible alternative.

Alex was wearying of what he thought of as the Uncommitted Lovers' Shuffle—the constant shifting between staying at his place or Casey's. He wanted to ask her to move in with him. The logistics would be simple enough, since her furnished rental was a month-to-month arrangement, but his apartment seemed so unworthy of her.

For the first time since his divorce he thought about the luxurious North Vancover house he'd sunk everything he'd earned into, only to sign it over to JoBeth along with all its contents and most of his other assets when she'd hit him with her idea of a fair settlement. He hadn't cared about the financial setback. Starting over had been an adventure, a rush of freedom, a relief from six years of trying to make his wife happy with endless acquisitions. As he'd told Casey, he'd felt so guilty about his failure as a husband, about the way he'd neglected JoBeth for his career, about compromising her budding social prominence by doing stories critical of some of the very people she'd been cozying up to—hell, he'd have given her anything if it would have salved his conscience.

Lately, however, he was wondering about all that guilt. He didn't experience it with Casey. Any of it. Ever. They had battles royal, but he was never left feeling like a selfish, uncaring bully who had no idea how to please a woman. Usually, in fact, he found himself feeling like a sometimes difficult but reasonably lovable male who knew exactly how to please a woman—the right woman.

But thanks to having taken the path of least resistance with JoBeth, he had nothing to offer Casey but an upstairs apartment in a broken-down old house, with furniture he'd barely looked at before carting it home. He was confident his situation was going to improve soon, and he knew Casey didn't care about that sort of thing. But *he* cared.

Since he didn't feel free to ask Casey directly to live with him, Alex found himself broaching the subject obliquely, chatting about his long-range plans for moving his newspaper operation to more officelike headquarters, eventually setting up his own printing facilities, and investing in a total renovation and restoration of the decrepit mansion.

Casey invariably lapsed into silence and wouldn't take his penny for her thoughts.

One sunny August morning at The Starting Gate, where he and Casey still joined Brittany most days for breakfast and often a brisk seawall walk, he made the mistake of wondering aloud whether his house was, after all, a white elephant.

The entire group landed on him with a vengeance.

"A white elephant!" Brittany said. "The Somerset's around the same age. Would you call it a white elephant?"

"My Smiley's not much younger than that building of yours," Ruby put in, stretching the truth by a few decades for the sake of making a point. "And let me tell you, handsome, he's worth preserving."

"True," Smiley agreed placidly.

"How could you say such a thing about that wonderful old house?" Casey asked, looking at Alex as if she suddenly wasn't sure she'd ever seen him before.

"What are *you* talking about?" he shot back. "You've said yourself that the place is weird."

"It's very weird. That's what makes it so wonderful." She made a face at him. "Kind of like you, boss."

Brittany laughed and got to her feet. "I believe I'll make my exit and let you two fight this one out on your own. I have to get to work early today. Good luck, Scoop," she said as she breezed out the door.

"Why does everybody always wish me good luck when Strawberry and I start in on each other?" he grumbled, though he was secretly pleased by Casey's reaction to his comment. Maybe she didn't think the old place was so bad.

But later, as the two of them strolled through the dew-sparkled park paths toward Casey's apartment so she could change from her jeans and sweatshirt to her working clothes, she was curiously silent again.

"A dollar," Alex suddenly said.

Casey tilted her head to one side and gave him a quizzical smile. "What did you say?"

"A dollar. Ten dollars. A C-note. I'll pay anything to find out what's going through your mind."

To his surprise Casey blushed.

"Make that a cool thousand," Alex said, draping his arm around her shoulders. "Just what are you thinking about?"

"Nothing," Casey said too hastily.

He tightened his arm and bent his head to murmur close to her ear, "You might as well tell me, sweetheart. If you don't, I'll coax it out of you in bed."

Casey's blush intensified. "The maddening thing is, we both know you could!"

Alex grinned. Casey did have a way, he thought happily, of making him feel like The World's Greatest Lover. "So shoot, honey. Get whatever it is off your chest."

"Okay, here goes," she said at last. "I feel I've learned enough about the weekly newspaper business . . ." She paused, worrying at her lower lip while carefully choosing her next words.

Alex slowly removed his arm from around her and shoved his hands into his jeans pockets, feigning nonchalance. But he felt as if someone had pulled the park lawn out from under him. All he could think of was that Casey was about to say she was ready to move on. But how could she consider such a thing?

It didn't make sense! "I'm not sure whether it's ever possible to learn enough about this business," he said carefully, "but I guess you're the only one who can make that decision."

"What I mean is," Casey went on, "I've learned enough to know what I really want and don't want."

Now what the hell did that mean? He braced himself for the worst while hoping for the best. "And what is it you've discovered you want or don't want?"

Casey paused again, determined now to say what she had to say, but to say it right.

The moments seemed endless to Alex, yet he managed to remain silent. A bird perched on a birch branch overhead trilled a song of pure, manic joy. Alex gave it a dirty look. Didn't the feathered fool know something serious was happening right under its beak?

"I've come to realize," Casey finally went on, "how incredibly naive I've been."

"Naive?" Alex repeated, a razor edge to his tone. "In what way?" While Casey hesitated yet again, her potential replies stampeded through his mind like bargain hunters shoving their way into a department-store sale. Was she going to tell him his windmill tilting was more trouble than it was worth? Was she about to confess that she missed the good old days when she made a maximum of money with a minimum of hassle? Or . . . would she tell him that she'd leapt into the relationship with him too quickly, that she wanted to cool things a little, think it over awhile?

Glancing at Alex, Casey frowned at the return of the muscle working furiously in his jaw. She hadn't seen that kind of tension in him for some time. Had he guessed somehow what she was about to suggest? Was he getting his back up about it without giving the idea any consideration whatsoever? "Look, I'm just not ready," she blurted out.

"For what?" Alex demanded. "Say it, will you? Get it over with!"

"For owning my own paper!"

Alex stopped dead and gaped at her.

Casey walked a few more paces, then turned to face him. He seemed surprised by her confession. Perhaps he didn't know what was coming after all. "I'm not sure I'll ever be ready," she added quietly. "I love the business, but to go it alone . . . I don't think so."

"But your dream, Casey," Alex said, hardly daring to hope.

She smiled, walked back to him, and took his two hands in hers. "A very wise man told me, not long ago, that life has a way of making us adjust our dreams as we go along. I've adjusted mine . . . a little."

"A little?"

Casey drew a deep breath and let it out very slowly. The moment of truth had arrived. "When Ron hired me," she said in measured syllables, "he mentioned that he and some of your other key employees have been allowed to purchase a few shares in the company, and . . . well, I have my nest egg, remember? I thought . . ." When Alex simply stood looking at her, his expression stunned, Casey started talking faster, eager to get in her whole argument before he automatically refused. "A quick infusion of cash would put Pacific Northwest Publications in a stronger position, wouldn't it? I know you're missing out on big profits every single week by using an outside printer. With all the papers in your chain, you should have your own facilities. I realize you're close to being able to handle that step, but if I could invest what I would have plowed into a—"

"Sweetheart," Alex cut in, at last finding his voice. "Oh, Casey, I can't believe this." The intensity of his relief was shocking to him even now, when he knew how much this woman meant to him. She wasn't about to leave. She wanted to link her future with his, at least professionally. She was prepared to go on beside him, tilting at windmills and all. "Baby, I can't accept your sweet, beautiful offer, but . . ."

"I knew you'd turn me down," Casey said with a disappointed glower. She stopped herself as she was about to stamp her foot. "Alex, just listen, okay? Be fair. Pretend I'm Ron, if that's what it takes to make you be objective about this. I'm not trying to horn in on your operation, but I believe in what you're doing. I believe in the future of this company. I believe in you. So why can't I buy shares? That way I'd have my dream, but it would be safer than if I tried to go it alone. I could keep working at *The Weekender* until you felt I was ready to run one of the smaller papers . . . or whatever. Any way you want it, Alex." She smiled tentatively. "My nest egg's not that huge. Not enough to give me the leverage to take over from you, boss."

The constriction in his throat didn't allow Alex to speak. He simply drew Casey closer, wanting nothing more than to hold her, to know she was still there for him to hold.

As he buried his face in her hair, Casey murmured, "Is this a yes?"

"No," he answered, then straightened up and smiled down at her. "No, Casey. I can't take your money. It would move things along faster, but I'll get there soon enough without risking the security you've worked and saved for. Just for the record, Ron and the others took their shares when they first started with me, as part of their salaries. By now, if things turn sour because of Jimmy Dawson or whatever, I can personally cover any losses they might suffer, but nothing more. The answer has to be . . . no."

All at once Casey felt like a fool. Whatever explanation Alex might give for his refusal, she was certain the real reason was an inherent implication of permanence in their relationship. She'd overstepped the limits. She'd been presumptuous. "Well, you wanted to know what I was thinking about," she said with a shrug, her tone brittle and her smile forced as she moved away from him. "It was just an idea."

Damn, Alex thought as they continued on their way in an uneasy silence. The nest egg. A little complication he hadn't thought about. Casey was so proud, so perverse, so touchingly insecure in her own odd way, she was thinking at this very moment that his rejection of her money was a rejection of her.

Since he was just as proud and perverse and insecure in *his* own odd way, he had no idea how they were going to bridge this idiotic gap that had opened up between them like the jagged fissure from a sudden earthquake. He only hoped the superficial damage wasn't an indication of a permanent fault line.

Eleven

Cecil Waters phoned Alex at ten o'clock that same morning.

At ten-fifteen Alex gathered *The Weekender* employees in the composing room. "We have a decision to make," he said quietly as he perched on one corner of Casey's worktable while she moved from behind it to stand with the others. "It's one that'll affect everyone here, so I want all of you to have your say." He paused to look at Casey to make sure she knew she was included. When she gave him an encouraging little smile, he went on, "I just heard from Bulldog." He shot another quick grin at Casey. "Cec Waters, that is. He's picked up a tip that there are proposals in the works for certain municipal expropriations in the West End—including this particular property."

"Why?" Ron asked amid a general buzz of consternation.

"Supposedly for a children's playground," Alex answered with a wry smile.

Marg scowled and shook her head. "On this site?"

"It's not at all suitable," Sandra put in.

"The operative word," Casey said, "is *supposedly.* Am I right, Alex, in presuming that the property will sit unused for a couple of years, at which time it'll seem like a—pardon the expression—a white elephant, and will be sold off to some developer? Jimmy Dawson, for instance?"

"That's the way Bulldog and I see it," Alex answered, intensely proud of Casey. As usual she'd done her homework. She knew how many similar shady deals Dawson Developments had been linked to in the past. And the tossed-off jibe about the white elephant was vintage Strawberry.

"What are you going to do?" Ron asked.

Alex blinked, then smiled inwardly, realizing that his thoughts kept drifting to Casey even at a moment of crisis in his business. Apparently he was getting his priorities straight at last. "We have a couple of alternatives," he answered. "The city would pay for the property, so we could take the money and run, either to set up in new West End quarters or to forget this area and concentrate on our other papers. Or we could fight."

"Darn right we could," Marg said firmly. "For one thing, we can get up a delegation to protest the expropriation."

"Good idea," Alex said, heartened by her reaction. "But we keep having to put out these little grass fires. It's Jimmy's way of trying to wear us down, I guess. If we're going to do battle, my feeling is that we come out swinging. And we can. Cec has been busy. He's put together a report showing all the secret Dawson holdings, all the questionable permits he's been issued, all the building codes he's circumvented. It's quite an eye-opener. If we print this stuff, we might rattle a few important cages. But things could get nasty. Jimmy could hit us with a libel suit, and even though every word is true, he could break us with court costs before we prove it. Or he could resort to . . ."

"Good heavens," Sandra said in her tiny, timid voice, "you don't think he'd be desperate enough to plant a bomb or anything, do you?"

Alex smiled and shook his head. "Jimmy's not a big-time crime boss, he's a two-bit thug. But I've always thought him capable of sending in a crew to bust up our offices. That's why I can't make this decision alone. In this instance I'll abide by the majority's will. And if you want time to think things over . . ."

"I'm for printing whatever you've got on Dawson," Ron cut in. "This is Wednesday, but if we really push, we can get it into this Saturday's paper."

"And meanwhile, I'll talk to Smiley and Ruby about getting that delegation together," Marg said, lifting her chin. "They're plugged into the neighborhood better than anyone."

There was a pause. Alex looked at Casey.

She scowled. "You have to ask, for heaven's sake?"

He laughed. "No, I suppose not."

Everyone's gaze went to Sandra.

"Well?" Marg prompted. "What do you say, Sandy?"

Sandra lifted her thin shoulders in a shrug, and the corners of her tremulous mouth turned up as she said sweetly, "I say we nail that sucker right to the wall."

By midnight Casey and Alex were so exhausted, they fell into his bed, too worn out even to make love despite the instinctive entangling of their naked bodies. They'd been writing and getting pictures and checking facts nonstop since the morning's meeting.

They were going to meet another deadline, but the two of them had taken the brunt of making sure of it.

"Hey, are we a team or what, Casey McIntyre?" he murmured as he cuddled her in the circle of his arms, her head pillowed on his shoulder, her palm flattened against his chest, her left leg bent at the knee and thrown comfortably over his thighs. "The whole crew, of course. But working with you is so easy, sweetheart. Things just get done. No ego . . ."

"Amigo," she said with a drowsy giggle.

"Together, wherever we go," Alex added, chuckling. Another silly rhyme from another old song. Absently stroking the long slope of Casey's hip and thigh, he felt her body relaxing into his, her breathing deepening with the beginnings of sleep.

The strained moments that had followed their early-morning discussion about her nest egg might never have happened, Alex realized with some astonishment. Granted, she'd taken a moment out of her hectic afternoon to go into his office and quietly tell him she'd been thinking about his refusal to let her invest and had realized she might feel the same way in his position. But even if she hadn't reached that point, Alex had a feeling they'd have been just as comfortable together now, just as happy, just as close. Casey had the unique gift of keeping individual disagreements and difficulties in a place apart, to be dealt with or not dealt with, but never to affect her overall feelings.

It occurred to him that she approached her relationship with her mother and father the same way: She didn't deny her disappointments and the unfulfilled longings, but she loved her folks as if they'd been model parents.

He remembered how she'd told him once about her former fiancé, and it suddenly seemed significant that she'd spoken with genuine fondness, as if the plan to get married had been an unfortunate near mistake that could have spoiled a wonderful friendship.

When Casey loves, she doesn't demand perfection, Alex thought, rapidly growing sleepy himself yet struggling to stay awake, knowing that a crucial truth was getting through to him at last. Casey's love was a force of nature, as unjudgmental and generous and inevitable as the opening petals of a flower or the spill of fast water over a sheer cliff into the crystal pool below.

When Casey loves, he thought again, another truth suddenly dawning.

Casey loved him.

He felt her soft breath against his skin. The silkiness of her inner thigh. The rhythmic rise and fall of her breasts, the steady beating of her heart.

All at once he understood everything that mattered. He'd been holding back because of not having enough to offer her, but there was only one thing he could give Casey that she would value. "Casey," he whispered, his lips brushing her forehead. "Casey, sweetheart, I love you too."

Casey stirred, pressed her lips to the center of his chest, and sighed. "Oh, good!"

She sat bolt upright as the morning sun streamed through the window. Sitting up on her haunches, she peered down at Alex. "What did you say?"

Alex swam up slowly from a deep, contented sleep. Bringing his arm up to shield his eyes against the light, he pried his eyelids open and saw the silhouette of a beautiful woman with a halo of golden hair.

And she was, he realized, his. All his. "I said I love you too," he answered.

"What do you mean *too*? Did I tell you I loved you? I do, of course, but did I say it?" Casey asked, her expression puzzled and her tone curious.

"Baby," Alex said as he reached for her, "let me count the ways."

"Say it again," Alex commanded as he and Casey walked back to *The Weekender* after a celebration dinner at the finest restaurant in the West End—The Rose Room at The Somerset. It was Saturday night. The edition with the Dawson exposé had been delivered without incident and was being snapped up at the newsstands, and Alex's mind was on other matters. It was a perfect summer evening, Casey looked lovely in an ultrafeminine confection of off-the-shoulder turquoise gauze and lace, and she loved him. "Say it, Strawberry," he persisted.

"I love you," Casey repeated as if reciting by rote. But as she looked at Alex and saw how genuinely happy he was, she couldn't keep up her teasing. Looping her arm through his, she said with renewed warmth, "I do love you, Alex. How could I not? You're fantastically handsome, for one thing." And he was, she thought as her glance swept appreciatively over his dark suit and the crisp white shirt that gleamed against his golden skin. "And you're brilliant," she went on. "Also brave, ambitious, kind to children and puppies, a pillar of your community, honest and upright and . . ."

"But do you think you could learn to care for me?" he interrupted.

Casey laughed. "Alex McLean, I've loved you forever and will love you forever. Got that, boss? I *love* you!"

Alex smiled. "You know, I'm beginning not to mind that *boss* thing quite so much."

"Then I'll have to put a stop to it," Casey shot back.

"Perverse brat."

"Closet tyrant."

"I love you, Strawberry."

She beamed at him. "I know."

"Speaking of closets," Alex said as they started along the familiar street to the office, "there are quite a few good-size ones in the old white elephant."

Casey stared at him, her pulse running wild. "What are you saying, Alex?"

He took a deep breath and mentally rehearsed the speech he'd prepared. "Just that we do seem to make such a terrific team, Strawberry," he said after a moment, "I was wondering if . . ." His words trailed off, and he stopped walking, then swore quietly.

Following the sudden direction of Alex's gaze, Casey froze.

Vic Lundstrom was sitting on the gray steps of *The Weekender* house.

Alex automatically turned to tell Casey to make tracks.

One look at her, and he realized there was no point. His gorillas were her gorillas. But damn, what if she got hurt?

"Vic's alone," Casey said. "Or appears to be. Strange . . . where's his crew?" Aware that Alex was waging a battle within himself between shooing her away and accepting whatever support she could give, she decided to make it easier for him. "Okay, boss. This one's all yours. I'll cover your back."

Alex couldn't help grinning. "You know, I have a feeling you'd like nothing better than to get caught in a saloon brawl. Casey McIntyre, soon-to-be-McLean."

His grin faded as he realized he'd just blown all his plans for a romantic proposal.

Casey forgot all about Vic Lundstrom as her head snapped around and she stared at Alex. "My oh my, you really *are* a bossy individual, aren't you?"

"It wasn't supposed to come out that way," Alex said, wincing. "I have champagne and roses waiting upstairs. But until we can deal with this latest ripple on the stormy sea of our life together, so that I can carry on with the proposal I'd planned, keep this thought in mind: You won't even have to change your monogram."

"I don't put monograms on things."

"Oh."

"However," Casey said as they carried on to face Vic, "I'm looking forward to the champagne and roses."

They reached the mansion's front walk, and Vic got to his feet.

"He's bigger than I'd remembered," Casey murmured. "And maybe the others are already inside, getting ready to smash a few objects and heads with baseball bats. In the event that we don't get through this one, boss, I'd like you to know the answer would have been yes."

"We'll get through it. You won't mind living in this weird old place?"

"I'll love it. But I hope you'll allow a woman's touch."

"As long as you're the woman whose touch we're talking about."

"McLean," Vic boomed. Big, brawny, his hair bleached almost white by the sun, he made Casey think of a Viking about to lay siege to a Saxon keep.

Stopping at the foot of the steps, Alex sighed. "What can we do for you this evening, Vic?"

"Your lady doesn't scare easy," Vic observed.

"I don't scare at all," Casey retorted.

He tipped back his head and roared with laughter. "McLean, I hope you know how lucky you are."

"If you're talking about my girl, I do know. If you're talking about anything else, maybe you could give me a hint," Alex answered guardedly.

Vic started down the steps. "I was talking about the lady. The rest isn't luck. The rest is guts. You don't scare easy, either. But you've created a little problem for yourself with that paper you put out today. Jimmy Dawson is not happy. He took one look at those stories you printed, and he ordered me to get my crew together and come over here to do some significant damage."

"I see," Alex said, as if Vic had said something perfectly reasonable.

Casey kept looking around, wondering where Vic's men were lurking.

"I told Jimmy," Vic went on, "what he could do with his orders. Me and the guys, we're supposed to be construction workers. I'm a professional. It's funny how you can forget things like that. You cut a few corners here, put on a little pressure there . . . you make excuses for yourself because you like the fat paychecks. But all of a sudden you get pushed too far, and you start thinking about things like being proud of what you do. So I decided to do something I could be proud of. I came over to tell you to hire some security for a couple of days. When you weren't here, I stuck around just in case Jimmy had found some-body else to do his dirty work. My crew won't, and that's a guarantee. We're all heading out to Calgary to sign on with an old buddy of mine. The guy plays it straight, and he needs some reliable help."

Alex gaped at Vic, then at Casey, then at Vic again. "So you came here to *protect* us?"

Vic laughed uproariously again. "Hell, no. You two can take care of yourselves. I was just . . . house-sitting, you might say." He glanced at Casey. "By the way, miss, young Marty's been feeling pretty sheepish about you."

"I hope he cools it with his drinking," Casey remarked. "That's his whole problem. Tell him he's going to pile up that 'Vette of his if he doesn't stay sober."

"He's already thinking about that, but I'll pass along the message," Vic said, his lips twitching with amusement. He thrust out his hand toward Alex. "I wouldn't count on official investigations of Dawson and the people he's paid kickbacks and bribes to, McLean."

"Why?" Alex asked, accepting the handshake though he was still discombobulated, not at all sure whether or not to trust Vic's change of heart.

Vic shrugged. "Jimmy was always careful to make sure his under-the-table doings would be tough to prove. Even if I'd be a witness against him—and I would—his lawyers could make mincemeat of anything I said. But things were coming apart for Dawson Developments even before you started in on him. You just made him desperate enough to get crazy. It's my guess Jimmy will be selling off his properties, closing down *The Gazette*, and leaving town so fast, he won't be around to read next week's letters to the editor. Hell, he was already shredding files when I left him."

Alex nodded, finally beginning to accept that Vic was on the up-and-up. "Well, I hate to see Dawson start all over somewhere else, but if getting him out of our backyard is the best we can do, it's better than nothing."

"Jimmy won't be starting anything for quite a

while," Vic said as he went down the walk to the street. "He blew himself right out of the water here." With a grin and a casual wave the Viking was on his way.

Alex turned to Casey. "I guess we should call Bulldog to put a watch on the place until we're sure it's safe."

"Definitely," Casey agreed. "After all, I'd hate to be interrupted during the champagne and roses by marauding newspaper busters." She watched Vic's departure, then shook her head. "The whole caper certainly seems to have ended so easily," she murmured.

Laughing, Alex said with mock concern, "Are you disappointed, sweetheart? Do you feel cheated of the dustup you were looking forward to?"

"Are you kidding? A person would have to be insane to want to tangle with that bruiser." Casey smiled at Alex as she walked over to him, twined her arms around his neck, and rubbed noses. "Anyway, I suspect I'll be enjoying more than my share of dustups over the next few decades. It'll be one of the bonuses of a lifetime spent with you. . . ." Her eyes twinkled with mischief as she added, "Boss."

Twelve

"Does Alex know?" Brittany asked in a hushed, almost reverent tone on a rainy Friday afternoon in April.

"Not yet," Casey answered excitedly. "That's why I asked you to come over. I couldn't keep it to myself any longer."

They were sitting cross-legged on the newly restored parquet floor of what had been the composing room of *The Weekender*, but was soon to be a gracious living room—as soon, at least, as Casey could settle on the dominant color theme for carpets and curtains. They were surrounded by wallpaper books, fabric and rug samples, and half-opened crates of furniture.

Brittany shook her head in disbelief. "How could Alex not know? You two are so close, you're like one person."

"I haven't had any nausea," Casey explained. "And Alex had been in and out of town, tearing around the other papers so much for the past few weeks, it's been amazingly easy to keep this one little secret from him."

"This one little secret," Brittany echoed, rolling her eyes. She looked down at the fanned-out samples. "Wouldn't it be more to the point for us to be choosing teddy-bear motifs and maybe an antique cradle? Good heavens, Casey, when are you going to give your husband the news?"

"This afternoon, as soon as he gets home from the office. He's going to be as thrilled as I am, so I didn't want to take even a slight chance of disappointment. I wanted the doctor's confirmation first." Casey picked up a small square of patterned wool carpet. "What do you think, Britt? You're so much better at this sort of thing than I am."

Brittany sighed and gave in. "Casey, all the choices you've narrowed down to are perfect, so you have to make up your own mind. You and Alex are the ones who'll be living with what you pick. What does he think?"

"He says I'm the boss," Casey answered disgustedly.

Brittany grinned. "Poetic justice. Serves you right." Looking over the samples again, she tried to be helpful. "How about cost? Can we eliminate any choices on the basis of being too expensive?"

"Not really. We're pretty well off these days, you know. It's incredible. All the papers are doing even better than Alex had projected—"

"Thanks largely to his wife's brilliant promotional and editorial ideas," Brittany cut in.

"That's what Alex says," Casey admitted, "but I don't agree. The solid foundation was there to work with. When he proposed, Alex was like a Victorian suitor describing his future prospects. He said he thought and hoped he was on the brink of big success but could just as easily go down the tube. It wasn't long before I realized he was being overly modest—and of course, once the threat from Jimmy Dawson was removed and the closing of *The Gazette* left the field clear for us. Alex suddenly became perfectly reasonable about letting me invest my nest egg in the company, which helped put us over the top. But the point is, Alex had laid the basis too carefully for things to go wrong. He'd worked so hard. . . ."

"Casey," Brittany said with an amused smile. "You're starting to sound like Marg and Sandra. Surely no man can be as wonderful as that husband of yours!"

"You wait, Britt. Just you wait until you find your other half. You'll be as sickening as I am."

"What's this?" a familiar male voice said. "What are you being sickening about, sweetheart?" Alex asked as he strolled into the room, coming home to his half-renovated house from the sleek new West End headquarters of Pacific Northwest Publications, a couple of blocks away.

Casey blushed and darted a surreptitious wink at Brittany, a silent message that certain things didn't have to be reported to curious husbands. "I'm being sickeningly indecisive about a simple matter of decorating," she grumbled.

He was dressed in casual clothes, so he hunkered down to sit on the floor with Casey and Brittany. "Go with the blue," he said after several moments of studying the samples.

Casey frowned. "I was leaning toward the rose."

"So the decision's made," he said complacently. "You prefer the rose. All you needed was me to argue with."

Laughing, Brittany leapt to her feet. "Thank heavens that's settled. Now I can get back to work."

Alex and Casey saw her to the door, and after she'd

left, he turned to his wife. "That was the fastest disappearing act I've seen since Jimmy Dawson's. Was it something I said?"

Casey suppressed a grin. "May I see you in your office, Alex?" she asked, turning on her heel to stride into the restored dining room that was in the same chaotic state as the living room.

As she whirled to face him, it was all she could do to keep a straight face. His utterly puzzled expression was priceless.

"What did I do now?" he asked with mock concern.

Casey went to him, took his hand, and gently flattened it over her stomach. "Boss honey," she said softly, "you have no idea."

THE EDITOR'S CORNER

As winter's chilly blasts bring a rosy hue to your cheeks and remind you of the approaching holiday season, why not curl up in a cozy blanket with LOVESWEPT's own gift bag of six heartwarming romances.

The ever-popular Helen Mittermeyer leads the list with **KRYSTAL,** LOVESWEPT #516. Krystal Wynter came to Seattle to start over in a town where no one could link her with the scandalous headlines that had shattered her life. But tall, dark, and persistent Cullen Dempsey invades her privacy, claiming her with an intoxicating abandon that awakens old fears and ensnaring her in a web of desire that keeps her from running away. A moving, sensual romance—and another winner from Helen Mittermeyer!

LOVESWEPT's reputation for innovation continues as Terry Lawrence takes you right up to the stars with **EVER SINCE ADAM**, #517, set in an orbiting station in outer space! Maggie Mullins is there to observe maverick astronaut Adam Strade in the environment she helped design—not to succumb to his delicious flirting. And while Adam sweeps her off her feet in zero gravity, he fights letting her get close enough to discover his hidden pain. Don't miss this unique love story. Bravo, Terry, for a romance that's out of this world!

Please give a rousing welcome to Patricia Potter and her first LOVESWEPT, **THE GREATEST GIFT,** #518. Patricia has already garnered popular and critical success with her numerous historical romances, and in **THE GREATEST GIFT** she proves her flair with short, contemporary romance, as well. Writing about a small-town teacher isn't reporter Lane Drury's idea of a dream assignment—until she meets David Farrar. This charming rogue soon convinces her she's captured the most exciting job of all in a romance that will surely be a "keeper." Look for more wonderful stories from Patricia Potter in the year to come.

Let Joan J. Domning engulf you with a wave of passion in **STORMY'S MAN**, LOVESWEPT #519. Gayle Stromm certainly feels as if she's in over her head with Cass Starbaugh, who's six feet six inches of hard muscles, bronzed skin, and sun-streaked hair. Gayle's on vacation to escape nightmares, but caring for the injured mountain climber only makes her dream of a love she thinks she can never have. Cass can't turn down a challenge, though, and he'd do anything to prove to Stormy that she's all the woman he wants. An utterly spellbinding romance by the incomparable Joan J. Domning.

Marvelously talented Maris Soule joins our fold with the stirring **JARED'S LADY**, LOVESWEPT #520. Maris already has several romances to her credit, and you'll soon see why we're absolutely thrilled to have her. Jared North can't believe that petite Laurie Crawford is the ace tracker the police sent to find his missing niece, and, to Laurie's dismay, he insists on joining the search. She's had enough of overprotective men to last a lifetime, yet raw hunger sparks inside her at his touch. Together these two create an elemental force that will leave you breathless and looking for the next LOVESWEPT by Maris Soule.

IRRESISTIBLE, LOVESWEPT #521 by beloved author Joan Elliot Pickart, is the perfect description for Pierce Anderson. This drop-dead-gorgeous architect thinks he's hallucinating when a woman-sized chicken begs him to unzip her. But when a dream girl emerges from the feathers, he knows the fever he feels has nothing to do with the flu! Calico Smith struggles to resist the sensual power of Pierce's kissable lips. She's worked so hard for everything she has, while he's never fought for what he wanted—until now. Another fabulous romance from Joan Elliott Pickart.

And (as if these six books aren't enough) LOVESWEPT is celebrating the joyous ritual of weddings with a contest for you, a contest that will have three winners! Look for details in the January 1992 LOVESWEPTS.

Don't forget FANFARE, where you can expect three superb books this month. **THE FLAMES OF VEN-GEANCE** is the second book in bestselling Beverly Byrne's powerful trilogy. From rebellion plotted beneath cold, starry skies to the dark magic that stalks the sultry Caribbean night, Lila Curran's web, baited with lust and passion, is carefully being spun. Award-winning Francine Rivers delivers a compelling historical romance in **REDEEMING LOVE**. Sold into sin as a child, beautiful, tormented "Angel" never believed in love until the strong and tender Michael Hosea walked into her life. Can their radiant happiness conquer the darkest demons from her past? Much-acclaimed Sandra Brown will find a place in your heart—if she hasn't already—with **22 INDIGO PLACE**. Rebel millionaire James Paden has a dream—to claim 22 Indigo Place and its alluring owner, Laura Nolan, the rich man's daughter for whom he'd never been good enough. Three terrific books from FANFARE, where you'll find only the best in women's fiction.

As always at this season, we send you the same wishes. May your New Year be filled with all the best things in life—the company of good friends and family, peace and prosperity, and, of course, love.

Warm wishes from all of us at LOVESWEPT and FANFARE,

Nita Taublib

Nita Taublib
Associate Publisher, LOVESWEPT
Publishing Associate, FANFARE

FANFARE

Rosanne Bittner

_____ 28599-8 EMBERS OF THE HEART . $4.50/5.50 in Canada
_____ 29033-9 IN THE SHADOW OF THE MOUNTAINS
$5.50/6.99 in Canada
_____ 28319-7 MONTANA WOMAN .... $4.50/5.50 in Canada

Dianne Edouard and Sandra Ware

_____ 28929-2 MORTAL SINS .... $4.99/5.99 in Canada

Tami Hoag

_____ 29053-3 MAGIC .... $3.99/4.99 in Canada

Kay Hooper

_____ 29256-0 THE MATCHMAKER, ... $4.50/5.50 in Canada
_____ 28953-5 STAR-CROSSED LOVERS .. $4.50/5.50 in Canada

Virginia Lynn

_____ 29257-9 CUTTER'S WOMAN, ... $4.50/4.50 in Canada
_____ 28622-6 RIVER'S DREAM, ... $3.95/4.95 in Canada

Beverly Byrne

_____ 28815-6 A LASTING FIRE .... $4.99/ 5.99 in Canada
_____ 28468-1 THE MORGAN WOMEN .. $4.95/ 5.95 in Canada

Patricia Potter

_____ 29069-X RAINBOW .... $4.99/ 5.99 in Canada

Deborah Smith

_____ 28759-1 THE BELOVED WOMAN .. $4.50/ 5.50 in Canada
_____ 29092-4 FOLLOW THE SUN .... $4.99/ 5.99 in Canada
_____ 29107-6 MIRACLE .... $4.50/ 5.50 in Canada